CW01501843

Backrooms The Caretaker's Journal

Backrooms

Fandom Books and Michael Schuerman

Published by Fandom Books, 2023.

BACKROOMS THE CARETAKER'S JOURNAL

First edition. October 27, 2023.

Copyright © 2023 Fandom Books and Michael Schuerman.

ISBN: 979-8223669647

Written by Fandom Books and Michael Schuerman.

The Caretaker's Journal: Chronicles from the Backrooms

Introduction

To whomever stumbles upon this journal,

It's odd, penning an introduction when I'm uncertain anyone will ever read this. It feels like sending a message in a bottle into an endless ocean of yellow, hopeful that someone, somewhere, will find it and know they're not alone in this maddening labyrinth.

I am the Caretaker. That title was not one I chose, but one that was thrust upon me. As days blurred into nights, and nights into days, I took it upon myself to maintain a semblance of order amidst the chaos of the Backrooms. I've swept floors, dusted off antiquated furniture, and tended to the remnants of lost souls who've unfortunately met their untimely end here.

But my job isn't solely about cleaning. No, it's more about witnessing – observing the ever-shifting rooms, the haunting whispers, and the terrifying entities that lurk just beyond the corner of one's vision. The very walls here pulsate with memories, with stories begging to be told. And I've become the reluctant chronicler of these tales.

Contained within these pages are my observations, my encounters, my fears, and, on rare occasions, my hopes. They're a testament to my time spent navigating this boundless maze, a guide for the next wanderer who might need it.

Do remember, not everything here is as it seems. The Backrooms are deceptive, ever-changing, and at times, brutally indifferent. But with every twist and turn, every narrow escape, every eerie silence, there's a lesson to be learned. An understanding of this place's enigmatic rules.

If you're reading this, perhaps you too are trapped within these walls. Or perhaps, by some twisted stroke of fate, this journal has found its way outside, a tangible piece of an intangible realm. Whatever the case may be, let this be a beacon for you. A glimmer of knowledge in the darkness.

Hold on to hope, stay vigilant, and may you find your way, as I continue to search for mine.

With an ever-watchful eye,

The Caretaker (1 of Many)

Entry 1: *Finally settled into the job, but what kind of a job did I stumble upon, I also found my first corpse today.*

Finally settled into the job. The stagnant yellow light and the hum of fluorescent bulbs feels oddly soothing. Found my first corpse today, leaned against a corner. Mummified by the dry air, I guess.

The day I stepped into the role of caretaker for the Backrooms, I did not know what to expect. All the stories, the rumors, the whispered tales of endless corridors and rooms that stretched beyond comprehension - they paled in comparison to the reality that greeted me.

The air here is still, suffused with a silence that is almost palpable. The endless expanse of monotonous yellow walls and the dull, patterned carpet beneath my feet provide little comfort. Yet, there is a certain serenity in this sameness, a rhythm in the monotonous hum of the fluorescent lights that have become my constant companions.

As I made my rounds, navigating through the labyrinthine maze of corridors and rooms, I stumbled upon a sight that cemented the reality of my new occupation. Propped against a corner, in a room that seemed no different from the countless others, was a body. A person once alive, now reduced to a mummified husk, a silent testament to the cruel nature of this place.

The dry air of the Backrooms had preserved the body in a haunting state of suspended decay. The features were still discernible - a man, perhaps in his thirties, with a look of perpetual surprise etched onto his withered face. His clothes, though faded, suggested he was not a relic of the distant past. The realization that he, like me, might have been a wanderer, a lost soul trying to find a way out, sent a shiver down my spine.

I approached cautiously, a mix of morbid curiosity and a sense of duty propelling me forward. In his hand, clutched tightly even in death, was a small notebook. Gently prying it open, I found pages filled with scribbled notes, drawings of what appeared to be maps, and desperate messages to loved ones he would never see again. It was a chilling reminder of the fate that befell many who found themselves lost in this forsaken place.

As the caretaker, it was my responsibility to remove the remnants of those who had succumbed to the Backrooms. I did so with a solemn reverence, aware that this man, like me, had stories, dreams, and a life beyond these yellow walls. With each step I took to carry him away, I felt the weight of the task I had undertaken. It was not just about maintaining the eerie order of this place, but also about honoring the memories of those who had traversed these corridors before me.

As I laid him to rest in a designated area, a part of me wondered about his story, about the choices and twists of fate that led him here. I wondered too about my own path, the sequence of events that led me to become the caretaker of this endless, enigmatic expanse.

With the day's task completed, I found myself drawn back to the hum of the fluorescent bulbs, the only constant in a world where time and space seemed fluid and unpredictable. Despite the foreboding atmosphere, there was an odd sense of calm that settled over me. Maybe it was the acceptance of my role, or perhaps it was the beginnings of an understanding of the Backrooms and its mysterious ways.

As I retired to my quarters, a small, sparsely furnished room much like the others but with the addition of a modest bed, I couldn't shake off the feeling that this was just the beginning. That there were countless stories etched into the walls of this place, waiting to be uncovered. And so, with a pen in hand and a resolve to document my journey, I began the first entry in what would become an extensive chronicle of my time as the caretaker of the Backrooms.

*Entry 2: **It's not just the dead you find here. Sometimes, I stumble upon old notes, journals, or scribbles on the walls. Hints of hope, or the desperation of someone trying to find a way out.***

The dimly lit corridors felt like they were alive, breathing softly and echoing with whispers of the long gone. The flickering lights cast eerie shadows that danced and played tricks on the eyes. Every creak of the floorboards, every rustle of paper, sent prickles down my spine. This was a place where reality intertwined with the surreal.

But as days melded into one another, the seemingly unending monotony began to crack, revealing hidden layers. While the dead were a grim constant, the Backrooms also bore silent testimonies of those who once treaded here, of their stories, and of their futile attempts to escape.

The remnants of the lost were scattered in the most unlikely places. I'd find torn pages crammed into crevices of decaying wood, or journals left behind on moldy shelves, their pages swollen with moisture. Scribbled notes, often half-faded, littered the floors, each a fragmentary glimpse into someone's torment or hope.

One chilling message, written in red – I shuddered to think if it was ink or something else – read: "Can you hear them too? The whispers? They promise freedom, but all they bring is madness." Another note, written in frantic, hurried letters, said: "They watch from the shadows. Don't trust the lights."

As I ventured deeper, the walls seemed to close in, their surfaces marred with countless attempts at communication. Makeshift calendars, perhaps a desperate attempt to mark the passage of time, were etched beside hastily drawn maps with circled areas and cryptic symbols. Amidst these symbols, one recurring image stood out: an eye, often crossed out, as if warning of a watcher or some lurking presence.

While tales of despair were abundant, glimmers of hope weren't entirely absent. A diary, its leather binding cracked and pages yellowed, belonged to someone who believed they were close to a solution. It detailed a series of rooms and hallways that, if followed correctly, promised an exit. The last entry, however, was abruptly cut off, leaving me wondering about its author's fate.

But not all entries were analytical. Some were maddened ramblings, speaking of walls that breathed, shadows that whispered, and lights that lured wanderers into traps. The consistent theme was the danger of trusting anything in the Backrooms. Even time itself seemed treacherous here, with some notes suggesting days had felt like years.

The weight of these stories pressed heavily upon me, but they also provided a purpose. I began collecting these artifacts, preserving them in a room I dubbed "The Archive." This somber sanctuary became a testament to the human spirit, its tenacity, and its inevitable fragility.

Sitting amidst these countless tales, an overwhelming sensation would often wash over me. A melancholic connection to the authors, an understanding of their fears, hopes, and the sheer will to survive. It was a haunting reminder that in the depths of the Backrooms, the line between hope and despair, reality and illusion, was perilously thin.

Entry 3: *Heard something lurking in the distance today. Slow, deliberate footsteps. I hid in a room, waiting for it to pass. Close call.*

The nature of the Backrooms was such that silence was as oppressive as any sound. The ceaseless hum of fluorescent bulbs became a haunting lullaby that seemed to echo the heartbeat of this cursed place. But today, that silence was shattered.

As I meandered through a particularly winding corridor, a chilling sound pierced the air. At first, I thought my mind was playing tricks, as it often did in this place of endless yellow and muffled echoes. But then, it came again: the unmistakable sound of footsteps. Not the hurried, panicked footfalls of a lost soul, but slow, methodical steps – deliberate and purposeful.

A cold dread seeped into me. This was no lost wanderer; it was something else, something I had only heard whispered tales of. Instinctively, I searched for a hiding place, ducking into an adjacent room that seemed untouched by time. The wallpaper was peeling, revealing patches of mold underneath, and a thick layer of dust had settled on the floor, disturbed only by my own hurried footprints.

I crouched behind an old, moth-eaten sofa, my heart pounding so loudly I feared it would give away my position. As the footsteps grew closer, they were accompanied by another sound – a dragging noise, as if something was being pulled along the floor. My mind raced with terrifying possibilities. Every shadow became a potential threat, every creak a sign of impending doom.

The room's only source of light, a flickering bulb overhead, cast eerie patterns on the walls, making it seem as if they were closing in on me. And then, something even more unsettling happened: the bulb began to dim, slowly plunging the room into a deep, impenetrable darkness. Only the sound remained – the footfalls now right outside the door.

I held my breath, praying it wouldn't sense my presence. Moments felt like hours, but eventually, the footsteps and the dragging sound moved past the door, growing fainter and fainter. When I could no longer hear them, I waited even longer, not daring to emerge from my hiding place.

When I finally mustered the courage to leave, the hallway outside was empty, save for a new mark on the floor. A long, wet streak, starting from where I had first heard the sounds and disappearing around a distant corner. The implications were clear: something was roaming these hallways, and it was not alone.

The rest of the day, every sound put me on high alert. The previously mundane hum of the lights now seemed to hide whispered secrets. The once-familiar corridors felt more menacing, as if eyes were watching from every shadowed corner.

This place, I realized, held more horrors than just the despair of the lost. There were entities here, lurking in the unseen, waiting for the unwary. Today had been a close call, a stark reminder that the Backrooms were a realm of unpredictability, where safety was an illusion and danger lurked just beyond the veil of the known.

*Entry 4: **Found a shrine today. Small figurines, candles. Looked fresh. Made an offering just to be safe.***

The geometry of the Backrooms is an enigma. Corridors twist and turn upon themselves, and rooms exist within rooms, each more confounding than the last. But today, my aimless wandering led me to a place unlike any other I'd encountered in this yellowed maze.

It was a recessed alcove, not much larger than a closet. But what it contained sent chills down my spine. There, bathed in the sickly glow of the overhead lights, was a shrine. It was an unsettling sight amidst the otherwise drab and repetitive surroundings. Four intricately carved figurines stood in a semi-circle, their features grotesque and alien, yet eerily human in their expressions of pain and reverence.

The floor of the alcove was covered in a pattern of symbols, drawn in what looked like ash. At the center of these symbols was a bowl filled with an unknown, viscous liquid that shimmered oddly in the light. Surrounding the bowl were candles of varying sizes, some still burning with a flame that gave off no heat. Their wax had dripped onto the symbols, suggesting recent use.

Curiosity pushed my fear aside momentarily, and I leaned in to inspect the figurines. Each was unique, crafted with meticulous detail. One had multiple eyes covering its entire face, another bore limbs that twisted into impossible angles, and yet another seemed to be melting, its form dripping like wax. The final figure was the most unsettling: it was featureless, save for a gaping, tooth-filled maw where its face should be.

The sight was deeply unnerving, but what truly alarmed me was the realization that this shrine looked fresh, recently tended to. Someone, or something, had been here not long before me.

Recalling tales of olden times, where offerings were made to appease vengeful spirits or curry favor with deities, I felt an impulse to leave an offering of my own. Perhaps it was the sheer oppressiveness of the Backrooms, the sense of being constantly watched and pursued, that made me believe that a gesture, no matter how small, might grant me some protection or goodwill.

Rummaging through my pockets, I found a small trinket I had picked up days before — a silver locket without a photograph. With a hesitant breath, I placed it in the bowl, amidst the strange liquid. Almost immediately, the room's temperature seemed to drop, and the overhead lights flickered violently before steadying.

Whether it was my imagination or a response to my offering, I couldn't tell. But as I backed away from the alcove, I couldn't shake off the sensation of unseen eyes upon me, scrutinizing my every move.

The rest of my journey that day was plagued by whispers that seemed to come from nowhere and fleeting shadows that darted just beyond the corner of my vision. The shrine, with its grotesque figurines and fresh candles, served as a haunting reminder that the Backrooms were not just a prison of endless corridors and rooms but also a dwelling place for entities unknown and perhaps best left undisturbed.

Entry 5: *Another body. This one was clutching a compass. Broken. I wonder if they thought it would help them navigate.*

The oppressive weight of the Backrooms was a constant. The never-ending corridors, the suffocating silence, the haunting hum of the fluorescent lights — it all served to remind those trapped within of the hopelessness of their situation. But nothing was more chilling than stumbling upon the remnants of those who had come before, a stark reminder of the fragility of hope and life in this distorted reality.

As I navigated through a particularly narrow corridor, I noticed a figure slumped against the peeling yellow wallpaper ahead. Drawing closer, the familiar stench of decay assaulted my nostrils, signifying another unfortunate soul who had succumbed to the Backrooms.

The body was that of a middle-aged man, his face twisted in a grimace of despair. His attire suggested he might have been an adventurer of sorts — sturdy boots, a utility belt filled with empty pouches, and a frayed backpack lying discarded by his side. But what truly caught my attention was what he clutched in his rigor-mortised hand: a brass compass.

Carefully prying it from his grasp, I examined the object. The glass face was shattered, and the needle, which should have pointed north, spun aimlessly, unable to find its bearing. It was as if the very laws of physics were defied within the walls of the Backrooms, rendering such tools useless.

I pondered the thoughts that must have raced through the man's mind. Had he entered the Backrooms intentionally, compass in hand, believing he could map out and navigate this bewildering maze? Or had the compass been a last-ditch effort, a desperate hope clung to when all else seemed lost?

As I continued my exploration, the broken compass weighed heavily in my pocket — a symbol of the futility many felt within this place. The very walls seemed to mock the efforts of those who believed they could understand or conquer the labyrinthine expanse.

Whispered taunts echoed faintly, reminding me of the countless souls who had tried and failed.

Further down the corridor, I discovered another eerie sign of the man's journey. Scrawled on the walls were lines and arrows, attempting to chart a path. Yet, the drawings spiraled into madness, looping back on themselves, revealing the unraveling sanity of their creator.

The shadowed recesses of the Backrooms hid many horrors, from the unseen entities that stalked the hallways to the psychological torment that wore down even the most resilient minds. The man with the compass had been just another victim, his faith in a simple navigational tool turned to despair as the very fabric of reality seemed to warp around him.

The compass, though broken and useless, became a poignant artifact of my collection, a reminder of the eternal struggle between hope and despair that played out in the echoing chambers of the Backrooms.

Entry 6: *I saw her again. The woman in the white dress. She never notices me, always just out of reach, wandering aimlessly.*

The repetitive sameness of the Backrooms can play tricks on the mind. Infinite stretches of nondescript yellowed corridors can make one believe that they're walking in circles. However, there's a different kind of repetition that has started to haunt my days — the recurring sight of a mysterious woman dressed in white.

It began a few weeks into my tenure as the Caretaker. I had been mapping out a new area, marking the walls discreetly to keep track of my progress. As I turned a corner, a flash of white caught my eye. There, at the end of the hallway, was a woman. She had long, flowing dark hair that contrasted starkly with her pristine white dress, which billowed around her as if caught in a gentle breeze — though no wind existed in the Backrooms.

Curiosity piqued, I called out to her, but she seemed not to hear, drifting into another corridor. I rushed forward, hoping to catch up, but she was always just a turn ahead, her presence marked only by the soft rustling of her dress.

Over the subsequent days, sightings of the woman in white became more frequent. Each time, I'd attempt to approach, to offer aid or establish some form of communication. Yet, each attempt was futile; she remained forever out of reach, seemingly oblivious to my presence.

Her spectral appearance began to take on an eerie significance. Was she a fellow wanderer, trapped in this endless maze? Or was she something else — a manifestation of the Backrooms itself, or perhaps a residual echo of someone long gone?

In one particularly chilling encounter, I found myself in a room with faded wallpaper depicting a serene lakeside scene — an oddity in the usual drabness. As I surveyed the room, the woman emerged from the shadows, her image reflected in the still waters of the wallpapered lake. For a brief moment, our eyes met in the reflection, and I could see the deep wells of sorrow in her gaze. But as soon as I blinked, she vanished, leaving only the silent waters behind.

I began to search for signs of her passage — a discarded item, a message, or any other trace. All I ever found was the occasional imprint of a bare foot on the dusty floors or the faintest scent of jasmine in the air. These fleeting traces only deepened the enigma.

Whispers among the notes and journals I'd collected spoke of apparitions, of shadows and entities that haunted the Backrooms. Some were to be feared, while others, like the woman in white, were more enigmatic. Several accounts mentioned seeing her, each with a similar refrain: she was always just out of reach, her true nature and intentions unknown.

As days blurred into one another, the woman in white became a constant, an anchor in the shifting unreality of the Backrooms. Whether she was a beacon of hope, a warning, or merely another piece in the puzzle, I couldn't tell. But her presence, ethereal and elusive, served as a haunting reminder of the countless souls who had walked these halls, their stories intertwined in the fabric of this place.

Entry 7: *Some rooms are colder than others. Some have that unmistakable smell of decay. Avoided one today that reeked of death.*

While the Backrooms were a seemingly endless expanse of similar-looking corridors and rooms, not all of them were identical in nature. Some carried unique characteristics, peculiarities that made them stand out in the relentless maze. One such variation was the temperature.

In my wanderings, I began to notice that certain rooms held an unnaturally cold temperature. As if stepping into a freezer, these rooms would send an immediate shiver down my spine, the breath visible in the air. But the coldness wasn't the only distinction — it was the feeling, an overwhelming sensation of being watched, an unease that permeated the very air.

This particular day began like any other. My routine of marking the walls, collecting remnants of lost souls, and avoiding any audible threats remained unchanged. As I ventured into a new section, however, I was met with an icy blast. The sudden drop in temperature was immediate and unmistakable. My breath clouded in front of me, and every sound became muffled, absorbed by the chilling atmosphere.

Approaching the door to the cold room, I noticed a layer of frost forming around its frame. It seemed out of place, considering there was no discernible source for such cold. Curiosity urged me to explore further, but as I reached for the doorknob, a pungent aroma hit me — the unmistakable, gut-wrenching smell of decay.

Hesitating for a moment, I pressed my ear against the door, listening for any signs of movement. All I could hear was a distant, rhythmic dripping, like water droplets echoing in a vast cavern. Against my better judgment, I cracked the door open slightly, just enough to peek inside.

The room was shrouded in darkness, the usual overhead lights either broken or dimmed. In the weak light filtering in, I could make out shapes — furniture covered in thick layers of frost and, more disturbingly, silhouettes on the ground. Several of them. Bodies, sprawled in unnatural positions, their final moments of despair evident in their frozen postures.

But what truly chilled me to the bone wasn't the sight of the deceased. It was the shadows that danced at the edge of my vision, flitting between the bodies, seeming to feed off the cold and the death.

I quickly shut the door, feeling a wave of nausea wash over me. The room, with its sinister cold and smell of decay, was a testament to the unpredictable nature of the Backrooms. It was a place where death lingered, where the very walls seemed to absorb the despair and pain of its occupants.

Retreating from the area, I made a mental note to mark it, to warn any potential wanderers of the dangers within. But as I moved further away, a chilling thought gripped me — how many more such rooms existed in this infinite maze? And what other horrors lay hidden within their depths?

The cold room remained an ominous reminder that, in the Backrooms, danger lurked around every corner. And that some doors were best left unopened.

Entry 8: *A surprise today! A room full of clocks, all ticking but none in sync. Made me lose track of time, but I found another note. "Follow the clocks," it read.*

The Backrooms, with their incessant uniformity, rarely offered any respite from their droning monotony. However, on occasion, there came moments that stood out, rooms that broke the mold. Today, I stumbled upon one such aberration.

I could hear it before I saw it. A soft, rhythmic ticking, growing steadily louder as I approached the source. As I stepped through the doorway, I was met with an astonishing sight. The room was filled, wall to wall, with clocks. Grandfather clocks with their stately pendulums, cuckoo clocks awaiting their hourly pronouncement, elegant mantle clocks, and even some that looked like they belonged to another era altogether. Each ticked away, but none matched the rhythm of the other, creating a chaotic symphony of misaligned time.

The room, bathed in a dim golden hue from the ancient-looking light fixtures, exuded an otherworldly charm. The shadows cast by the clocks' hands danced on the walls, creating an ever-changing tapestry of patterns. It was oddly entrancing. The relentless ticking lulled me into a trance, and I found myself wandering aimlessly amidst the horological wonders, each tick and tock a whisper from a bygone era.

However, it wasn't long before I realized a disconcerting fact — I had no idea how long I'd been in there. The mismatched cadence of the clocks, each telling a different time, disoriented my senses. Time, it seemed, played by different rules in this chamber.

Pushing down the rising panic, I tried to retrace my steps, to find the door through which I'd entered. But the endless rows of clocks disoriented me further, their chimes and ticks morphing into a cacophonic maze.

Just as despair began to set in, my foot brushed against a piece of paper on the ground. Picking it up, I strained to read it in the dim light. The note, scrawled in hurried handwriting, read: "Follow the clocks."

The ambiguous message did little to soothe my nerves. What did it mean to follow the clocks? Did it refer to a specific clock, a specific time, or perhaps a direction? My eyes darted around, searching for any hint or clue.

Then, I noticed it. One of the clocks, an ornate grandfather clock with intricate carvings, was out of place. Unlike the others, its pendulum swung in a distinct pattern, seeming to point in a specific direction with each swing. Intrigued, I approached it and, upon closer inspection, found a faintly glowing path on the floor, leading away from the clock.

With little else to guide me, I decided to take a leap of faith and follow the illuminated trail. It meandered through the maze of ticking contraptions, leading me to a door concealed behind a wall of clocks.

Stepping through, I was met with the familiar sight of the monotonous Backrooms corridors. While I was relieved to be out of the clock-filled room, the enigma it presented lingered in my mind. Who had placed the clocks there? What was the purpose of the note? And were there more such chambers, each holding a clue or a challenge?

But those questions would have to wait. For now, I had a new lead to follow and an ever-growing mystery to unravel. As I ventured forth, the rhythmic ticking from the clock room continued to echo in my ears, a haunting reminder of the fluidity of time in this perplexing realm.

Entry 9: *They're getting closer. The monsters. I can feel them, sense their hunger. Left more offerings today.*

There's an intangible aura the Backrooms exude, a constant hum of energy that makes your skin crawl. Yet, with time, even that unnerving sensation becomes a background noise, something to be acknowledged but ignored. Today, however, the ambiance shifted. The oppressive stillness was punctuated by an unseen malevolence, a presence that sent chills down my spine.

It began subtly, shadows seeming to move just at the edge of my peripheral vision. Each time I'd turn to look, there'd be nothing but the familiar decaying yellow wallpaper and the droning fluorescent lights. I tried to dismiss it as my imagination, a result of prolonged isolation in this maze of despair. But as the day progressed, the fleeting glimpses grew more frequent, more tangible.

Whispers danced around me, ethereal and disembodied. Low growls, incoherent murmurs, and the soft padding of feet echoed in the distance. Each sound seemed to come from all directions, making it impossible to discern their origin. The monsters of the Backrooms, entities spoken of in hushed tones and scribbled notes, felt nearer than ever.

I had heard of them, of course. Every wanderer who'd been trapped in this endless expanse had their tales — stories of elusive creatures that stalked the corridors, always lurking but seldom seen. Until now, I had considered myself fortunate for not having crossed paths with them. But today, their encroaching presence was undeniable.

Determined to keep them at bay, I began scouring my surroundings for offerings. It was rumored that these creatures could be placated, albeit temporarily, with tokens of appeasement. My findings were meager — a few tarnished coins, an old wristwatch with a cracked face, a faded photograph of a couple, and a half-eaten candy bar. I laid them out methodically in a small clearing, hoping it would be enough.

Sitting in the gloom, I waited, watching the shadows play tricks on the walls. Time seemed to stretch indefinitely, the minutes morphing into hours. And then, as if on cue, the atmosphere shifted once more.

From the darkness emerged forms, nebulous and ever-changing. They circled the offerings, their forms flickering like old film reels. Some appeared humanoid, their faces a blur of features, while others were more abstract, amorphous blobs of darkness. They moved silently, their intentions inscrutable, examining each token with what seemed like curiosity.

Minutes passed, or perhaps it was hours, before they began to retreat, fading back into the void from whence they came. The room felt lighter, the oppressive weight lifting ever so slightly.

While I had staved them off for now, the encounter served as a grim reminder of the constant peril the Backrooms posed. It wasn't just the maze-like corridors or the mental toll of isolation that threatened one's sanity. It was the unknown, the lurking dangers that could emerge from the shadows at any moment.

Drawing a shaky breath, I made a mental note to always be prepared, to gather more offerings and always be on guard. For in the Backrooms, the line between reality and nightmare was perilously thin, and one could never be too careful.

Entry 10: *I heard laughter today. Faint, distant, but unmistakably human. Another survivor or just my imagination playing tricks?*

In the never-ending silence of the Backrooms, any sound that breaks the monotony can feel like a lifeline, a connection to a reality that seems increasingly like a distant dream. Today, that lifeline was the sound of laughter.

It was so unexpected, so out of place in this desolate labyrinth, that at first, I thought I had imagined it. The sound was faint, barely audible over the incessant hum of the fluorescent lights. A gentle, melodic laughter, echoing through the endless corridors, bouncing off the stained walls and threadbare carpets.

I stopped dead in my tracks, straining my ears, trying to pinpoint the direction from which it came. It seemed to drift from everywhere and nowhere, a disembodied chorus that played hide and seek with my senses.

For a moment, hope surged within me. Could it be another survivor? Someone else trapped in this purgatorial existence, a fellow wanderer in the maze? The thought propelled me forward, my footsteps quickening as I tried to chase down the elusive sound.

But as I ventured deeper, the laughter began to change. What started as a sound that hinted at humanity soon twisted into something else. The once melodious laughter morphed into a cacophony of cackles, mocking and sinister. It no longer sounded human, but rather like a cruel mimicry of joy, distorted and warped by the Backrooms' twisted reality.

My heart raced, pounding against my chest as I realized that this was no fellow survivor. The corridors seemed to close in around me, the laughter growing louder, more oppressive. It was as if the very walls were laughing at my naivety, at the fleeting hope I had dared to harbor.

Panic set in, and I found myself running, my footsteps echoing in the empty halls. The laughter pursued me, a relentless specter that seemed to revel in my fear. I didn't stop until my lungs burned and my legs ached, until the laughter had faded into a haunting whisper that lingered in the air.

Exhausted, I collapsed against a wall, my breath coming in ragged gasps. The silence that followed was suffocating, heavier than before. I realized then that the Backrooms were not just a physical trap but a psychological one as well, preying on the mind, feeding on hope and fear alike.

As I sat there, regaining my composure, I couldn't help but wonder if the laughter had been real or just another cruel trick of this place. Had there been a moment of genuine human connection, however brief, or was it merely a figment of my starved imagination?

One again the next day It started as a mere whisper, a soft giggle that seemed to float on the air. Thinking I might have imagined it, I stopped in my tracks, straining to hear more. But there it was again, louder this time, the unmistakable sound of laughter. It was light and melodic, reminiscent of a child's innocent mirth.

Every instinct told me to follow it, to seek out its source. Perhaps, against all odds, there was another soul trapped in this desolate realm. Or could it be a sign, a beacon leading to an exit or safe haven?

As I ventured deeper into the maze, the laughter continued, playing a tantalizing game of hide and seek. At times it felt close, almost within arm's reach, while at others it seemed to drift away, receding into the vastness of the Backrooms.

The further I went, the more the environment began to change. The monotonous yellow walls gave way to decaying wallpaper with patterns of faded roses, the floors turned from cold linoleum to creaky wooden boards, and the buzzing lights were replaced by flickering chandeliers casting eerie shadows.

It felt like I had stumbled upon an older part of the Backrooms, a section long forgotten and overtaken by time. Here, the atmosphere was even more oppressive, the weight of countless lost souls pressing down on me.

The laughter grew more pronounced, now accompanied by other sounds — the distant clinking of glasses, soft murmurs of conversation, and even faint music. It was as if I was approaching a gathering or celebration.

Then, abruptly, I found myself standing before a grand ballroom. Its grandeur was a stark contrast to the rest of the Backrooms, with ornate pillars, shimmering chandeliers, and a vast dance floor. But what truly caught my attention were the figures.

Spectres of men and women, dressed in period clothing, waltzed across the floor, their movements graceful yet eerily silent. Their faces were blurred, devoid of features, but they exuded an aura of joy and revelry.

In the midst of it all, a young girl in a white dress stood, her laughter the very sound I had been following. She beckoned to me, her intentions unclear, but her presence strangely comforting.

However, before I could approach her, a chill ran down my spine. The realization hit me — these weren't survivors or benign spirits. They were echoes of the past, remnants of those who had been consumed by the Backrooms, their final moments replayed in an endless loop.

Backing away slowly, I exited the ballroom, the laughter and music fading behind me. The encounter left me rattled, a poignant reminder of the deceptive nature of the Backrooms. While it offered glimpses of hope and connection, it was all too often a mirage, a trap set to ensnare the unwary.

Entry 11: *Found a mirror room. Avoided looking at my reflection. Last time I did, it...moved differently.*

Among the many terrors and oddities of the Backrooms, few spaces unnerved me as much as the mirror rooms. They were relatively rare, interspersed throughout the infinite labyrinth like a cruel joke, designed to prey on the vulnerability of those who encountered them.

Today's discovery was unexpected. As I wandered through a nondescript corridor, I was caught off guard by the sudden brightness. An entire room, bathed in an intense white light, its walls lined with floor-to-ceiling mirrors. I hesitated at the entrance, memories of my previous encounter flooding back.

The first time I stumbled upon such a room, curiosity had gotten the better of me. I had approached one of the mirrors, eager to see my own reflection after what felt like an eternity. But what I witnessed defied logic. My reflection had been... off. While I stood still, it moved on its own, mirroring my actions but with a slight delay, like a video lagging behind. Its eyes, cold and lifeless, stared back at me with an intensity that made my skin crawl.

Remembering that experience, I took a deep breath and cautiously edged along the room's perimeter, careful to keep my gaze averted from the mirrors. The room seemed to pulse with a malevolent energy, the air thick with tension.

Yet, as I moved, I couldn't help but catch glimpses of my reflection in the periphery. To my horror, I noticed that my doppelgänger was no longer lagging. Instead, it seemed to anticipate my movements, moving before I did, as if guiding or luring me.

Drawn into its hypnotic gaze, I found myself inching closer to one of the mirrors. My reflection's smile grew wider, its eyes gleaming with an unsettling glee. And then, in a hushed, distorted version of my own voice, it whispered, "Come closer."

I recoiled in horror, the sinister allure of the room breaking. My heart raced as I stumbled backward, desperate to escape its confines.

But as I turned to leave, a chilling realization gripped me: the room's exit had vanished.

Panic surged through me. Trapped in this reflective prison, I could feel the weight of countless eyes watching, waiting. The oppressive silence was broken only by the soft whispers of my reflections, their voices growing louder, their intent clear.

Summoning every ounce of willpower, I focused on the memories of those I had lost, the notes and stories I had collected, and the mission that drove me forward. Drawing strength from these memories, I approached the central mirror, my reflection's malevolent grin now replaced by a look of surprise.

With a determined yell, I shattered the mirror with a swift kick, the glass cascading to the ground in a glittering shower. As the shards fell, the room's oppressive energy dissipated, and the exit reappeared.

Breathing heavily, I made my way out, vowing never to be ensnared by the mirror room's allure again. The Backrooms were a place of constant peril, but it was encounters like this that served as stark reminders that the most dangerous battles were often fought within one's own mind.

Entry 12: *Had to move three bodies today. All of them seemed to have been running from something.*

The day began as most did in the Backrooms - an unending haze of yellowed walls and the persistent hum of fluorescent lights. Yet, as I trudged through the winding hallways, a scene of chaos unfolded before me.

Three bodies lay strewn across the corridor, each in varying stages of decay. Their faces, contorted in sheer terror, told a story of frantic flight and a pursuit by something relentless. Shoes worn out and clothes tattered, they had clearly been running for a considerable distance.

The first body, a middle-aged man, still clutched a ripped map in his hand. Faint sketches and hastily written notes covered the paper, hinting at an attempt to decipher the labyrinth's enigmatic layout. Nearby, a young woman lay sprawled, her fingers rigidly gripping a tarnished locket, its chain tangled around her wrist. The third, an older gentleman, had a notebook tucked into his jacket, its pages filled with symbols and diagrams, as if he had been trying to decode some hidden pattern within the Backrooms.

Gently, I began the somber task of moving the bodies to a designated area I had set up for such unfortunate souls. It was a quiet space, away from the central corridors, where I tried to lay them to rest with some semblance of respect. As I did, I couldn't help but wonder what had chased them. The Backrooms were home to many inexplicable phenomena and malevolent entities, but the sheer terror evident on their faces suggested something particularly sinister.

As I pondered, a chill ran down my spine. A distant echo, like the soft patter of feet, reached my ears. It was rhythmic, growing louder with each passing second. I squinted into the dimness, and for a fleeting moment, thought I saw shadows darting in and out of the periphery.

Not wanting to find out what lurked in the darkness, I hastened my efforts. With the bodies relocated, I quickly set up a perimeter of salt and lit a few candles, makeshift barriers I'd learned could deter some entities. Sitting quietly, I waited, listening intently.

The footfalls grew nearer, the air thickening with an oppressive energy. Suddenly, the temperature dropped, my breath forming misty clouds in the cold air. A dense fog rolled in, obscuring my vision and muting the omnipresent hum of the lights. Shapes seemed to move within the fog, amorphous and indistinct, like nightmares made manifest.

Then, just as suddenly as it had begun, the sound ceased, replaced by an unsettling silence. The oppressive atmosphere lingered, however, as if the air itself were heavy with anticipation.

Hours or perhaps minutes passed – time was always fluid here – before the fog began to lift and the familiar hum returned. The threat, it seemed, had passed.

Emerging from my makeshift sanctuary, I retraced my steps to where I had found the bodies. Strewn across the floor were dozens of black feathers, each glistening with an unnatural sheen. They were cold to the touch, and seemed to absorb the light around them, casting small pools of darkness on the faded carpet.

A reminder, if one was needed, of the ever-present dangers that lurked in the shadows of the Backrooms. Whatever had chased those poor souls remained a mystery, but the evidence left behind suggested it was a force to be reckoned with. A shiver ran down my spine as I collected the feathers, storing them in a cloth bag. They might hold some clue or, at the very least, serve as a warning.

Entry 13: *I wonder if the monsters were once lost souls like us, transformed by this place.*

The labyrinthine expanse of the Backrooms stretched out endlessly in every direction. The consistent drone of the overhead lights and the musty scent of old carpets became almost comforting in their predictability. But in this eerie stillness, a thought took root and festered in my mind, a thought more terrifying than the monsters themselves: Were these creatures once human?

The possibility that they might have been people, with dreams, aspirations, and families, transformed into grotesque beings by the unyielding nature of this place, filled me with dread. Were these entities, which now stalked me in the gloom, once explorers who had wandered into the Backrooms, or perhaps even caretakers like me, sworn to watch over the corridors but eventually consumed by their mind-warping vastness?

While making my way through a particularly dim section, I discovered a room unlike any other I had encountered. The entrance was heralded by an arched doorway, its wood darkened with age and etched with intricate patterns that seemed to shift and move when viewed from the corner of one's eye. Inside, the room was bathed in an otherworldly blue glow emanating from luminescent fungi that dotted the walls.

At the center of the room stood a massive table, its surface carved with countless names. Among them, to my horror, I recognized a few from the annals of those who had once been caretakers like me. Beside each name was a detailed drawing of a creature, some vaguely humanoid, others completely alien in form. The implication was clear—each caretaker, after succumbing to the madness of the Backrooms, had been transformed into one of the very entities they once sought to elude or control.

Leaning against the table was an ornate, dusty tome bound in what appeared to be leather. Tentatively, I opened it, revealing page after page of handwritten entries. Each was an account of a caretaker's experiences, their struggles, and ultimately, their transformations.

One entry in particular caught my attention:

"Day 527: The boundaries between reality and the illusions of the Backrooms blur with each passing day. My sleep is haunted by visions of elongated limbs and faceless entities whispering promises of eternal torment. I fear I am on the brink of becoming what I have always feared. If anyone finds this, know that once I was like you, a guardian of these twisted halls. But this place... it changes you, consumes you, until there's nothing left but the monster within."

As I continued to leaf through the pages, an unsettling realization washed over me. The lifespan of a caretaker in the Backrooms was not indefinite. Sooner or later, the relentless nature of this place would wear them down, stripping away their humanity and molding them into one of its own.

Suddenly, a bone-chilling wail echoed through the room, causing the luminescent fungi to dim momentarily. The familiar feeling of being watched returned. Swiftly closing the tome, I made my way back to the entrance, the weight of the knowledge I had gained pressing down on me.

The Backrooms were not just a trap for the unsuspecting but also a crucible, reshaping and molding those within its confines. Whether I would find an escape or become another entry in that grim tome remained to be seen, but one thing was certain: the line between man and monster was perilously thin in this place of endless hallways and lurking shadows.

Entry 14: *Found another note. This one had a map drawn in shaky lines. Marked a spot with an X.*

Despite the blinding light, a deep-rooted instinct within me refused to be consumed by it. This wasn't an ordinary room transition. No, this was the Backrooms challenging my resolve, my purpose.

Shutting my eyes tight, I mentally anchored myself, focusing on the core of my being, my identity. Memories rushed back—of how I became the Caretaker, of the many souls I'd encountered, and of the anomalies I'd faced. With each recollection, the blinding light dimmed, replaced by the familiar hum of the fluorescent lights and the musky smell of the yellow wallpaper.

When I finally dared to open my eyes, I found myself standing in the familiar maze of the Backrooms, the colossal wooden door now shut tight behind me. I approached it again, cautiously. To my surprise, the carved faces seemed different—less menacing, more contemplative—as if acknowledging my resilience.

A realization washed over me. The note, the 'X', the massive door—this wasn't a mere diversion but a test, an initiation. The Backrooms wasn't simply a random, malevolent force; it was sentient in its own twisted way. By challenging its inhabitants, it sorted out the wanderers from the protectors, the lost souls from the guardians.

And as its Caretaker, it was not just my duty to maintain order but also to prove, time and again, my commitment to this role. My hands, no longer trembling, reached out to touch the door, feeling the intricate carvings. A silent pact was made. I would continue to navigate its labyrinthine halls, not as a prisoner, but as a steward.

I retreated from the door, folding up the crumpled map and placing it securely in my pocket. The note, with its vague promise of an escape or something more, was but one of the many enigmas the Backrooms held. As I moved forward, the path seemed a bit clearer, the weight on my shoulders a touch lighter.

Yet, the whispering voices continued, some cautionary, some encouraging. They became a part of my journey—a testament to the many souls that had traversed these halls. Some, like me, might have taken on the mantle of guardianship, while others may have succumbed to the depths of despair.

With renewed purpose, I strode forward, the buzzing lights above casting their familiar glow. The Backrooms and I shared an unspoken bond—a relationship of mutual respect. As its Caretaker, I would ensure its mysteries remained, while its capricious challenges kept me vigilant, reminding me of the importance of my role in this ever-shifting realm.

Entry 15: *Bad day. Ran into one of them. Had to hide in a room for hours. Left it an offering of an old watch I found. Hope it appeases.*

The incessant hum of the fluorescent lights above had long become the soundtrack to my existence. Yet today, that ambient noise was interspersed with the guttural growls of one of "them." It was a sound I'd come to dread, a harsh reminder that the Backrooms were never truly safe, even for the Caretaker.

As I ventured deeper into a lesser-known section, the atmosphere grew palpably denser, the lights dimming intermittently, casting long, looming shadows. My instincts screamed danger, urging me to turn back. But curiosity, that ever-persistent drive, compelled me forward.

It wasn't long before my caution was rewarded with the sight of one of the entities—a twisted, gangly creature, its form barely held together by the sheer will of the Backrooms. It moved with a languid, erratic grace, its silhouette distorted and stretched, seemingly phasing in and out of reality.

Panic surged within me. My breath caught in my throat as I quickly backtracked, slipping into a nearby room. The door creaked shut behind me, the room itself offering little more than a heavy, old desk and the remnants of past wanderers—a discarded shoe, a rusted key, and an old pocket watch with its hands frozen in time.

In the distance, the creature's growls grew louder, more insistent, as if it could sense my presence nearby. Desperation clawed at my insides. I needed a plan, an escape. Then, an idea dawned. Perhaps, like ancient gods and monsters of old, this creature could be appeased with an offering.

Carefully, I wound up the old pocket watch, its ticking echoing eerily in the confined space. Taking a deep breath, I edged towards the door, placing the watch just outside, hoping its rhythmic ticking would distract or, better yet, appease the entity.

I retreated to my hiding spot, heart pounding in my chest as I waited. Hours felt like days in the oppressive silence that followed, broken only by the steady ticking of the watch.

And then, a shift. The creature's growls subsided, replaced by an odd, almost curious, chittering sound. The weight in the air lifted slightly, the room's oppressive atmosphere giving way to tentative relief. As time passed, the creature's presence receded, drawn away by the watch's relentless ticking.

Emerging from my hiding spot, my knees weak with relief, I couldn't help but crack a weary smile. "I wonder if I get any PTO being the Caretaker," I mused aloud. "Because after today, I sure could use a vacation." The absurdity of the thought, juxtaposed against the surreal horror of my environment, brought a brief, albeit needed, moment of levity.

But as the last echoes of my laughter died down, the weight of my role settled back in. As the Caretaker, my duty was clear. Regardless of the challenges and terrors I faced, I was bound to these endless corridors, ensuring the stability of this twisted realm.

Entry 16: *Rooms are shifting more frequently now. Found a room filled with old TVs. All static, but one showed an exit sign.*

The very bones of the Backrooms were restless. The once-familiar labyrinth had taken on a life of its own, its hallways twisting and contorting more frequently, seemingly reshaping themselves with every step I took. Even as the Caretaker, this phenomenon was both fascinating and deeply unsettling. It was as if the very essence of the Backrooms was rebelling, asserting its dominance and challenging my presence.

I've traversed many a strange chamber in my time here, but today's discovery was peculiarly haunting. A heavy wooden door, swollen with age and moisture, led me into a cavernous room. It was filled wall-to-wall with old television sets. They ranged from ancient boxy monochrome sets to slightly more modern, albeit still outdated, models. Each was perched on a rickety stand, cords snaking towards outlets that seemed to grow organically from the mold-speckled walls.

All the screens, save for one, displayed the frantic dance of static—the familiar "white noise" that one might associate with a lost signal. Their collective hum was maddening, the room alive with the electric cacophony. But it was the lone deviant television that caught and held my attention.

Amidst the chaos of snowy screens, this particular set showed an image that seemed strangely out of place—a brightly lit EXIT sign. It was the kind one might see in a theater or a public building, its bold red letters stark against a white background. The screen flickered intermittently, the edges of the image warping as if being viewed through water or warped glass. But that sign, with its promise of escape or at least a brief respite, was hypnotic.

A thought nagged at the edge of my consciousness: was this a hint? A clue left by the Backrooms, or perhaps by a previous wanderer, pointing the way to an egress? Or was it just another cruel trick, a siren song designed to lead the unwary to their doom?

A sudden, whimsical thought then crossed my mind, "If there really is an exit, even a temporary one, could I duck out for a smoke break?" The sheer audacity of the idea made me chuckle. In this endless expanse of nausea-inducing yellow wallpaper and the constant drone of overhead lights, the simple pleasure of a cigarette seemed both ludicrous and tantalizingly appealing.

But then, a more sobering question followed: If I were to step outside, even for just a moment, would the Backrooms even allow it? Would they notice? Would the entities that lurk in the shadows sense the absence of their Caretaker?

While these thoughts raced through my mind, a soft static-filled whisper emanated from the TV with the exit sign. It was barely audible, a voice—or perhaps multiple voices—merged into one, saying, "Seek and you shall find... but at what cost?"

I took a step back, my skin prickling with unease. Whatever the meaning behind the anomalous television set, one thing was clear: the Backrooms were watching, listening, and they were full of secrets that challenged the boundaries of understanding.

With a mix of trepidation and resolve, I made a mental note of the room's location and ventured forth, pondering the cryptic message and the ever-elusive promise of escape. Whether a brief respite or a permanent exit, the allure was undeniable. But in the Backrooms, nothing was ever as simple as it seemed.

Entry 17: *Some corridors are endless. Some rooms loop back to themselves. But occasionally, a door leads to salvation...or deeper damnation.*

In the oppressive sprawl of the Backrooms, certain truths had become evident to me over time. Corridors that stretched endlessly, their final destinations forever hidden in a gloom that not even the fluorescent lights could penetrate. Rooms where doorways would trick you, leading you back to the very point of entry, creating an infuriating loop that toyed with sanity. But among these disorienting mazes, there existed rare anomalies—doors that promised something more, doors that hinted at either a brief respite or a plunge into deeper, darker corners of this enigmatic realm.

One of these doors, hidden behind a cascade of peeling, yellowed wallpaper, had opened up to a serene garden bathed in twilight. A realm so starkly contrasting the dingy corridors I had come to know. Birds, or at least entities that mimicked them, flitted about, their chirps a sweet symphony to the ears. Another door, far less inviting, had led to a chamber filled with clocks, each ticking out of sync, their discordant chimes creating a maddening cacophony that still haunted my dreams.

With every exit or entrance I encountered, a moral quandary tugged at my soul. Should I, as a beacon for the lost and weary, leave marks on the walls? Symbols, perhaps, that would guide future wanderers either toward safety or away from peril? The weight of responsibility was heavy. Every time I contemplated it, my role as the Caretaker bore down on me. I was a guardian, a sentinel, bound by an unseen covenant to maintain neutrality.

Today, in a particularly shadow-drenched corridor, I chanced upon another such door. Its dark wood was intricately carved with interwoven patterns that seemed to writhe and shift as I looked upon them. The handle, a cold iron serpent with gleaming emerald eyes, seemed to beckon. The lure was irresistible.

The room beyond was both breathtaking and terrifying. A vast, starlit expanse stretched out, the floor made of translucent glass that offered a view of an endless cosmic abyss below. Constellations unfamiliar to my eyes shimmered, while distant galaxies spiraled. Amid this beauty, however, there were darker spots, voids that seemed to suck in all light and hope. Entities, nebulous and shadowy, floated below, their forms ever-shifting, their whispers echoing with a hunger that sent shivers down my spine.

A singular stone pedestal stood in the room's center, atop which rested an ancient tome bound in leather that seemed...alive. The pages, when I dared to glance, were filled with languages unknown, but their intent was clear—these were the very rules and fabric of the Backrooms.

I could have spent an eternity in that room, deciphering its secrets. Yet, the thought of leaving a mark for others to follow weighed on me. Would guiding them to such knowledge be a blessing or a curse? In the end, as I stepped out and the door sealed behind, I chose inaction. My role, after all, was one of balance. The Backrooms would reveal themselves to those it deemed worthy, and for the rest, their paths would remain shrouded in mystery.

As I treaded further into the labyrinth, the thought persisted: salvation or damnation, the line was often blurred, and perhaps it was best for each soul to find their own way in this ever-changing maze.

Entry 18: *Lost my bag today. Had my supplies. Need to find it soon.*

The essence of being the Caretaker in the Backrooms is a peculiar dance of order within chaos. My cleaning cart, with its array of brushes, sprays, and cloths, was more than just a utility; it was an anchor, a symbol of the semblance of control I sought to maintain in a world governed by absurdity.

So when I awoke this morning, or whatever time it might have been in this place devoid of natural light, to find my cart missing, a profound sense of unease settled over me. The echoing hum of the fluorescent lights seemed louder, the endless corridors more daunting. My cleaning supplies were extensions of my role, my duty, and without them, I felt diminished, vulnerable.

At first, I wondered if my mind was betraying me. Had I simply misplaced it in the vast labyrinth? But deep down, a nagging suspicion grew. The entities, the very monsters that lurked in the shadowy recesses, were they mocking the Caretaker? I'd heard whispers, seen fleeting movements from the corner of my eye, and often felt their presence, observing, maybe even studying me.

With determination, I embarked on an exhaustive search, traversing the winding, repetitive hallways. Along the way, I stumbled upon a room I had never seen before: walls lined with mirrors, each reflecting a slightly altered version of reality. One mirror showed the cleaning cart, but as I reached out to touch it, my hand passed through the glass, ripples emanating from the point of contact. Another mirror displayed a version of me, but with hollow eyes and a twisted smile, mocking my desperate search.

Hours, or perhaps even days—time's flow was a fickle thing here—passed. Exhausted and on the brink of despair, I made my way back to my room, the one place that felt constant in this mad realm. And there, to my disbelief and relief, stood the cleaning cart, perfectly arranged, as if it had never been touched.

The realization hit me like a cold draft. Someone or something was playing games, reminding the Caretaker of his place within the hierarchy of the Backrooms. In any other circumstance, I might have been filled with dread or anger. But in that moment, standing in the dim glow, I couldn't help but smirk. It was a reminder that even in this eerie expanse, there existed a peculiar sense of humor—a dark jest shared between the realm and its guardian.

Determined not to be bested, I resolved to be more vigilant, to remember that even the Caretaker wasn't immune to the capricious whims of the Backrooms. And perhaps, somewhere deep within the maze, an entity chuckled at its own mischievous prank.

Entry 19: **Whispers all around me today. Echoes of lost souls? Or the monsters trying to confuse me?**

The unnerving stillness of the Backrooms was frequently shattered by sounds that defied explanation, and among them, the whispers held a special place in my consciousness. Today, they were relentless—soft murmurs that seemed to come from everywhere and nowhere, a symphony of hushed voices that threatened to drown out my own thoughts.

At times, the whispers were so faint, I questioned if they were real or just products of my overworked mind. But today, they crescendoed, rising in volume and clarity. Phrases emerged from the cacophony, disjointed and fragmented: "...lost forever...", "...don't trust the walls...", "...follow the light...".

Were these the echoes of those who'd wandered these endless corridors before me? The imprints of souls who'd met their fate within the yellowed walls and under the sterile glow of fluorescent lights? I had come across remnants of the lost before—notes, personal items, and on occasions, the unfortunate remains of those who couldn't escape. Were these whispers their final messages, forever looping in the ambient air of this cursed place?

Yet, another theory tugged at the edges of my mind. The monsters. Those elusive, menacing entities that seemed as much a part of the Backrooms as the wallpaper and linoleum floors. Was it possible that these whispers were their doing, an attempt to disorient and ensnare the unwary? Their presence was always felt, but rarely seen. Perhaps this was just another one of their insidious tactics.

Shaking off the creeping paranoia, I reminded myself of my duty. I was the Caretaker. Regardless of the origins of these whispers, I had responsibilities. The constant shift and change of the Backrooms meant regular upkeep was essential. Cleaning, rearranging, and, more grimly, the removal of the unfortunate souls who'd met their end within this vast expanse.

As I pushed my cleaning cart down a familiar stretch, I stumbled upon a sight that halted my progress: a body, lifeless, positioned as if in sleep. The individual's face was one of peaceful reprieve—a sharp contrast to the chaos surrounding us. Positioned by their hand was a small tape recorder. Curiosity piqued, I pressed play, and a voice, tinged with weariness, filled the air.

"Is anyone out there? I've been wandering for what feels like years. The whispers won't stop. They promise salvation, but I fear they lead to doom. If you find this, know that I..."

The message was cut short, the tape ending in a harsh, abrupt static. I sighed, feeling the weight of my role. Here was another soul to be tended to, another story to be added to the ever-growing annals of the Backrooms.

With a heavy heart, I prepared to move the body, reminding myself that while I couldn't save everyone, I could offer them a semblance of dignity in their final rest. The whispers continued, but I tried to push them to the background, focusing on my solemn duty.

Entry 20: *A child's shoe, bloodied. No sign of the child. I hope they made it out.*

The Backrooms held an endless capacity to surprise and disturb, even for someone who had seen as much as I had. The vast stretches of yellowed wallpaper and disorienting mazes had seen countless lost souls, but nothing prepared me for the sight that greeted me today—a small, solitary child's shoe, its once vibrant hue now marred by splatters of dark blood.

It was placed eerily in the middle of the corridor, almost ceremoniously, as if it was intentionally left there to be found. The size indicated the wearer could be no older than five or six. My heart ached at the thought. Children, with their inherent innocence and vulnerability, had no place in this hellish labyrinth.

I scanned the vicinity, half-expecting to find the young owner nearby, hiding in fear or worse. But the endless corridors returned only silence, their secrets locked tight behind the monotonous hum of the overhead lights.

A part of me hoped that the child had somehow managed to find an exit, a portal to safety away from this oppressive domain. But deep down, a nagging fear persisted: what if the child was still trapped, wandering alone and terrified, with the lurking horrors of the Backrooms ever present?

I felt a profound desire to help, to break my self-imposed rule of neutrality and seek out the young soul. Perhaps this was the one exception I could make, a deviation from my role as the impartial Caretaker.

But then, a chilling memory resurfaced. A few days ago, I had witnessed an unsettling apparition—a child-like figure, floating eerily a few inches off the ground. Its movements were unnatural, an almost dream-like glide, before it phased seamlessly through a solid wall. The image of the spectral child, with eyes that seemed devoid of life or recognition, stood in stark contrast to the bloodied shoe. Was there a connection? Or were these disparate remnants of the countless lost souls that populated the Backrooms?

Gripping the small shoe, I felt an overwhelming sense of responsibility. There was so much I did not know or understand about this place. The line between the living, the dead, and the transformed was often blurred. But one thing was certain: as the Caretaker, I was bound to these halls, to their stories, and to their tragedies.

Placing the shoe on my cleaning cart as a solemn reminder, I pressed on, the haunting image of the floating child etched into my mind. Whether it was a harbinger of doom or a lost soul seeking solace, I could only hope that, in time, I would find answers. Until then, the weight of the unknown, coupled with the tangible evidence of the child's shoe, added another layer to the ever-deepening enigma of the Backrooms.

Entry 21: *Today, the entire corridor was upside down. The ceiling became the floor. Strangest sensation walking on light fixtures.*

In the ever-shifting realm of the Backrooms, reality was as fluid as the wavering reflections in a murky pool of water. Today's aberration, however, took even my seasoned senses by surprise.

As I stepped into a new corridor, there was a brief moment of disorientation, akin to the dizzying sensation one experiences on a vertigo-inducing ride. And then, it all snapped into place: I was walking on the ceiling. Or rather, the ceiling had become the floor, and the floor loomed overhead. The yellowed wallpaper now stretched downwards, ending in the overhead lights that were now underfoot.

It was a bewildering, gravity-defying experience. The light fixtures, typically far above and out of easy reach, were now directly beneath my feet. Their cold, metallic surface was oddly sturdy, albeit with an occasional disconcerting flicker that sent ripples across my path. Each step emitted a soft buzzing sound, a unique blend of the fixture's electrical hum and the muted crunch of my weight pressing down.

Despite the initial shock, I soon discovered a silver lining: the lights, typically a challenge to dust and maintain due to their elevation, were now easily accessible. The small pool of light they emitted illuminated the space around in an eerie, almost ethereal glow, painting dancing shadows on the inverted walls.

Every so often, I'd spot a door handle hovering far above, now inaccessible. It felt as though the normal rules of the Backrooms had been upended, leaving me in a strange limbo of confusion. Yet, this topsy-turvy realm did grant me a unique perspective. Details usually missed, like small cracks in the fixtures or hidden markings on the upper recesses of the walls, now lay exposed.

But this newfound insight came with its challenges. More than once, I stumbled over a dangling wire or a protruding fixture, unaccustomed to the terrain's newfound hazards. And the disquieting feeling of seeing doorways on the ceiling, their darkened openings promising another step into the unknown, added an unsettling layer to the experience.

Throughout my journey, a thought kept recurring: Was this the Backrooms' way of testing my adaptability? Or perhaps it was a reminder that in this labyrinth, nothing was static, not even the very foundation upon which one walked.

After what felt like hours (or was it days?), I approached the corridor's end, a door frame lying horizontally in my path. Approaching cautiously, I braced myself, not knowing whether stepping through would right the world or plunge me further into disarray.

But as I crossed the threshold, a familiar sensation returned. Gravity asserted itself once more, and I found myself standing upright, the corridor now as it should be, with the ceiling far above. I paused, taking a moment to process the surreal experience, and to appreciate the odd advantages it presented. The Backrooms might be a place of eternal uncertainty, but as its Caretaker, each new challenge only deepened my connection and understanding of its enigmatic passages.

Entry 22: *I swear I saw sunlight today. Just a crack, a sliver. It gave me some new energy, I can't remember the last time I saw the sun.*

In the twisted labyrinth of the Backrooms, where time lost all meaning and one's senses were constantly blunted by the insistent hum of lights and the ceaseless maze of identical hallways, any deviation was a shock to the system. Today, that deviation was a slender sliver of sunlight piercing through a near-invisible crack in the ceiling.

It was odd, standing there, the single ray illuminating a patch of the grimy carpet, dust particles dancing within the beam. It looked so out of place, this tiny shard of the outside world, amidst the suffocating monotony of the Backrooms. For a moment, I was transported, memories of sunlit days, the scent of flowers, the feeling of warm rays on the skin—all came flooding back. How long had it been since I last experienced such simple pleasures? Too long, undoubtedly.

The sunlight instilled in me an unexpected surge of vitality, as if the mere presence of the outside world had recharged some dormant part of my spirit. As I basked in its limited warmth, I couldn't help but ponder its significance. Was it a mere structural flaw? Or was it, perhaps, a subtle beacon meant to guide or inspire lost souls?

My duty as the Caretaker meant that I was tasked with the maintenance and upkeep of the Backrooms. Technically, any breach, even one as harmless as this, was my responsibility to rectify. But as I stood there, absorbed in the ethereal glow, a moral conundrum presented itself. Should I seal off this aberration, returning the room to its intended dreary state? Or should I let it remain, a symbol of hope for any other lost wanderers who might chance upon it?

Images flashed through my mind—lost souls, much like myself, happening upon this room and experiencing the same surge of hope and memories. For many, this could be a pivotal moment, a small reassurance that there was still an 'outside', that not everything was lost to the eerie depths of the Backrooms.

On the other hand, if the monsters of this place, those horrifying entities that lurked in its darker corners, were drawn to the light, it could become a trap. A deadly lure.

After what felt like hours of contemplation, my decision was made. I would leave the crack undisturbed. Sometimes, in places as bleak as this, the smallest ray of hope can be the difference between perseverance and succumbing to despair. I made a small mark near the crack—a subtle sign for myself should I wish to return.

Resuming my duties with renewed vigor, I couldn't help but frequently glance back at the room, the faint ray of sunlight a persistent beacon in the back of my mind. It was a tangible connection to a world I once knew, and for now, it was enough to sustain me. In the morose echo chambers of the Backrooms, sometimes hope, no matter how fleeting, was the most potent tool for survival.

Entry 23: *Rain. Indoors. Pattering on the linoleum floors. Nothing surprises me anymore.*

The labyrinthine corridors of the Backrooms often felt like they existed outside of natural laws, a place where the familiar became alien and the expected was constantly turned on its head. Still, even by the standards of this eerie realm, today's occurrence was exceptionally bizarre: rain, pouring from an unseen source in the ceiling, cascading down upon the yellowed linoleum floors.

Each drop created ripples as it struck, the sound amplified in the otherwise silent hallway. The sound of rain, a sensation so intrinsically linked with the outside world, felt out of place here. The rhythmic patter of droplets took on a hypnotic quality, with the steady drumming echoing through the empty passages.

I glanced upwards, trying to discern the origin of the rainfall. The ceiling, as ever, was concealed by the soft glow of the omnipresent fluorescent lights, their luminescence creating a haze that obscured any point of origin. For a moment, I imagined a vast and open sky just beyond, a world where rain was just a precursor to rainbows and the soft chirping of birds.

But that fleeting dream was quickly banished by the reality of the Backrooms. Here, nature had no dominion. The rain, though visually and sonically familiar, felt off. It was colder, devoid of the fresh scent that typically accompanies a downpour. And its presence posed numerous questions: Was this another manifestation of the Backrooms' capricious nature? A quirk in its ever-shifting dynamics?

And then there was the matter of the blood.

The rainwater, as it flowed, began to mingle with deep-red patches on the floor, remnants of some prior gruesome event. The rivulets started to wash away the stains, creating macabre streams that painted a grim tableau. It was a stark reminder that, for all its strangeness, the Backrooms were not without their dangers.

I found myself oddly grateful for the rain's cleansing effect. The Caretaker's duty was to maintain, and while I had grown accustomed to the various quirks of this place, the persistent presence of bloodstains was a reminder of the horrors that lurked in the shadows. The rainfall, in its own twisted way, was assisting me in my duties.

Still, standing amidst the indoor downpour, a sense of unease crept over me. It was almost as if the Backrooms were adapting, evolving in response to my thoughts and needs. This notion was as comforting as it was terrifying.

After a while, the rain began to wane, tapering off until the hallway returned to its usual stifling silence. The freshly cleansed floor reflected the sterile glow of the lights above. The scent of the rain, that odd metallic tinge, lingered in the air.

Entry 24: *Ran into another caretaker today. We shared notes and went our separate ways. How many of us are there?*

In a place where time seemed to bend and twist upon itself, encounters with others were rare. The solitude of the Backrooms could weigh heavily on the psyche, with the isolation acting as both a blessing and a curse. But today, that solitude was broken by the unexpected sight of another Caretaker.

At first, I mistook him for one of the many oddities that roamed these halls. His appearance was haggard, with unkempt hair and a beard that suggested he had been here longer than I. His uniform, like mine, was stained with the many trials of this place—smudges of dirt, patches of dried blood, and a general weariness that seemed to seep into the fabric itself.

As our eyes met, a silent acknowledgment passed between us. No words were needed to convey the shared understanding of our roles and the burdens they entailed. With a nod, he gestured to a small alcove, and we found ourselves sitting opposite one another, the hum of fluorescent lights above serving as a steady backdrop to our impromptu meeting.

Drawing out a tattered notebook, the other Caretaker began to share his notes, revealing maps of corridors I had yet to traverse, notes on rooms to avoid, and even sketches of entities he had encountered. Some of the drawings sent shivers down my spine—creatures of nightmare, half-familiar yet twisted into grotesque parodies of their former selves.

In turn, I shared my findings, pointing out areas of interest and detailing my own experiences. Our notes, though varied, painted a similar picture: the Backrooms were vast, constantly shifting, and fraught with dangers both seen and unseen.

But the most haunting revelation came as we discussed the very nature of our roles. The other Caretaker confessed that, like me, he was uncertain of how long he had been in the Backrooms. Days, years, decades—it was impossible to tell. And like me, he sometimes questioned the reality of his role. Were we truly Caretakers, appointed to maintain order in this chaotic realm, or were we just another aspect of the Backrooms' twisted designs?

As our conversation drew to a close, a heavy silence settled between us. The enormity of our shared predicament hung in the air. How many Caretakers were there? Were there others, each navigating their own section of this endless maze, believing themselves to be the sole guardians of a place that defied understanding?

We parted ways with a simple handshake, the brief human contact a rare comfort in a place so devoid of warmth. Watching him disappear into the twisting corridors, I couldn't help but wonder if our paths would ever cross again.

Entry 25: *Found a room with doors upon doors upon doors. Which one leads out? Which one leads deeper?*

The Backrooms had always presented a labyrinthine puzzle of corridors and rooms, each with its own eerie ambiance and quirks. But nothing had prepared me for the spectacle I stumbled upon today: a vast chamber, unlike any I had seen before, with doors stretching as far as the eye could see. It was as if someone had taken the essence of a thousand hallways and compressed them into a single, vast expanse.

The floor, with its standard yellowed linoleum, seemed to stretch endlessly, while the ceiling—disturbingly high and shrouded in shadow—was lit sporadically by dim, flickering lights. But it was the walls that caught my attention. Every inch was lined with doors. Wooden doors, metal doors, doors with peeling paint, doors with ornate knobs, and some with no discernible means of opening. Some were close together, almost touching, while others stood isolated, their unique designs hinting at the mysteries that lay beyond.

A cold draft swept through the chamber, causing the hairs on the back of my neck to stand on end. The silence was palpable, save for the soft, distant whispers that seemed to emanate from every direction. Were they the voices of lost souls, trapped behind one of these countless doors? Or were they echoes of my own mind, grappling with the sheer impossibility of the scene before me?

Approaching one of the doors, I noticed a faint glow seeping through the cracks. Drawn by curiosity, I slowly turned the knob and was met with a chilling sight: a room entirely submerged in water, with floating debris hinting at its past occupants. Swiftly shutting the door, I moved to the next, which creaked open to reveal a dense, fog-covered forest, the twisted trees seeming to beckon me forward.

Each door unveiled a new realm, some wondrous, others horrifying. There were rooms filled with mirrors reflecting endless versions of oneself, rooms that seemed to defy gravity with furniture and objects suspended in mid-air, and rooms so dark that they seemed to swallow all light and hope.

Amidst the overwhelming choice, a pressing thought gnawed at my mind: Which of these doors might lead to an exit from the Backrooms? And conversely, which might drag one even deeper into its clutches, into realms more treacherous and alien?

The vastness of this "Door Room," as I had come to think of it, was both tantalizing and terrifying. Each threshold represented a gamble. And as the Caretaker, did I dare take that risk? Or was it my duty to remain, to warn others of the potential dangers and temptations that lay behind each door?

In the distance, I thought I heard a soft melody—a lullaby, perhaps, or the hum of a familiar tune. Was it another trick of this place, or a sign, a guidepost among the myriad of choices?

With a heavy sigh, I took out my notebook, sketching the layout of the Door Room and making notes on the doors I had explored. If I was to navigate this place, to understand its secrets, I needed to be systematic, methodical. And perhaps, in time, I would find the door that led out... or deeper into the enigma that was the Backrooms.

Entry 26: *The monsters are restless. I hear them whispering my name.*

There are aspects of the Backrooms that remain, even to me, a mystery. The monsters, or entities as I sometimes refer to them, are one such enigma. They range in form, from vaguely humanoid shadows to grotesque aberrations that seem to defy the very laws of physics. Their motivations, desires, and origins remain largely unknown, and in the silence of these yellowed corridors, their presence becomes an ever-looming reminder of the dangers that lurk just beyond the next corner.

Today, the atmosphere in the Backrooms felt especially charged, tense. The omnipresent hum of the fluorescent lights seemed to have an added layer, a whispering undertone that was impossible to ignore. As I moved from room to room, carrying out my duties, I became acutely aware that I was not alone. The whispers grew louder, more insistent. And to my growing horror, I could discern my own name being repeated over and over, as if chanted by a malevolent choir.

"Caretaker... Caretaker..."

Some of the entities, over time, have come to recognize me, to understand the nature of my role here. We have reached a sort of unspoken truce: a mutual respect borne out of necessity. They keep their distance, acknowledging my purpose, and in return, I offer them wide berth, avoiding any actions that might provoke them. But not all entities are so understanding.

As I moved deeper into a particularly decrepit corridor, the peeling wallpaper giving way to mold and mildew, I heard the distinct sound of footsteps echoing behind me. Turning, I caught a fleeting glimpse of a tall, slender figure, its form obscured by tattered rags. In its elongated hand, it held a knife, glinting menacingly under the dim lights.

A surge of adrenaline propelled me forward. The corridor twisted and turned unpredictably, and every so often, I would glance back, only to find the entity relentlessly pursuing, its whispers morphing into raspy laughter.

Suddenly, a door to my left burst open, revealing another entity, this one more recognizable. A hulking mass of shadow, its many eyes blinked in recognition. We had crossed paths before, and it had shown no aggression towards me. Now, it seemed to stand guard, blocking the path of the knife-wielding creature.

Seizing the opportunity, I darted down another hallway, putting as much distance between me and my pursuer as possible. After what felt like hours, I found a small room to hide in, catching my breath and attempting to calm my racing heart.

The monsters of the Backrooms are as diverse in their intentions as they are in form. Some view me with indifference, some with hostility, and yet others, perhaps, with a begrudging respect. It's a delicate dance of coexistence, punctuated by moments of sheer terror.

As I eventually ventured back out, I couldn't help but wonder: What binds these creatures to the Backrooms? And why do some seem almost protective, while others are driven by an insatiable malice? One thing was certain, in this ever-shifting maze, alliances could be as unpredictable as the layout of the rooms themselves.

Entry 27: *Recovered my bag. But something had rummaged through it.*

The simple, frayed canvas bag had been my constant companion throughout my tenure as the Caretaker. It carried an assortment of essentials: a flashlight with spare batteries, a journal filled with notes and observations, basic tools for quick repairs, and personal trinkets that anchored me to a time before the Backrooms.

Today started as routine as any other in this place, with the familiar drone of fluorescent lights overhead. Yet, as I ventured into a previously familiar section, an uneasy feeling gnawed at me. The corridor seemed...different. More oppressive, the shadows deeper. The whispers, too, felt closer, as if carried on a wind that should not exist in this stagnant space.

My unease heightened when I realized my bag was missing. Panic surged, my heart raced. That bag was more than just a collection of items—it was a lifeline, my tether to sanity. Retracing my steps, I searched every corner, every room, desperation mounting with each passing moment. The omnipresent yellowed wallpaper seemed to mock my every move, making each room indistinguishable from the last.

Hours—or what felt like it—later, in the midst of a room flooded with eerie green light, I spotted it. The bag lay abandoned in the center of the floor, its contents scattered haphazardly around it.

As I approached, the magnitude of the situation hit me. The bag wasn't merely dropped—it had been intentionally rifled through. My journal was opened to a page of recent entries, its pages creased. The flashlight lay several feet away, its beam casting odd angles on the walls. But most disturbing was the state of my personal items. A family photograph I had kept was torn in half, and a small locket was crushed, as if by tremendous force.

It felt like a violation, an intrusion into the sacred space I had carved for myself amidst the chaos. The realization that one of the entities had done this, had shown such targeted interest in my belongings, sent a shiver down my spine.

Gathering my things, I noticed a new addition: an object not of my possession. It was a crude doll, fashioned from strands of what looked to be human hair, its body bound with scraps of the same yellow wallpaper that lined the Backrooms. The doll's face was twisted into a grimace, a macabre mockery of a smile, and its beady eyes seemed to fixate on me with malevolent intent.

The message was clear: I was being watched, studied even. Whatever had gone through my belongings had left this...gift, a chilling reminder of the ever-looming presence of the entities. Perhaps it was a warning, or maybe an attempt at communication. Either way, the boundaries between the Caretaker and the inhabitants of the Backrooms had blurred just a little more that day.

With renewed caution, I continued my duties, all the while feeling the weight of unseen eyes upon me, and the silent threat they carried.

Entry 28: *Chalk marks on the walls. Someone's counting days...or years. I wonder if they found an exit.*

Every inch of the Backrooms felt like it told a story of isolation and despair. The monotonous landscape of decaying yellow wallpaper and cold linoleum floors occasionally bore witness to a narrative of the countless lost souls that wandered these endless corridors. But today, one such story struck me more profoundly than the rest.

I had entered a section of the maze that felt older, the air denser, as if the weight of time pressed upon it. The lights in this area were dimmer, their buzz more like a mournful lament than the typical incessant drone. I stumbled upon a particularly long corridor, its stretch so vast it almost seemed to converge at a distant vanishing point.

What caught my attention were the chalk marks. Neat, distinct lines grouped in sets of five were drawn upon the peeling wallpaper. They were everywhere, wrapping around the corridor as far as the eye could see. There were hundreds, if not thousands of them.

My initial assumption was that it was a way to mark a path. But as I observed more closely, the dreadful realization set in. This wasn't a trail—this was a tally. Someone or multiple individuals had been keeping track of time, marking the passing days, or possibly even years, in a desperate attempt to maintain some semblance of sanity amidst the boundless void of the Backrooms.

I followed the chalk marks, my fingers occasionally brushing against the crude lines, feeling the coarse residue of the chalk. The further I ventured, the more frantic the marks appeared. They began as meticulous and organized, but as they progressed, they grew more erratic, more desperate. Some areas were smeared as if the hand that drew them had been trembling.

Nestled between the lines, I occasionally found messages, fleeting snippets of thoughts scrawled with the same chalk:

"Is anyone there?"

"I hear them close."

"Lost track of time. How long? How long?"

The melancholy of this place, these writings, weighed on my heart. The author's despair, their sense of abandonment, resonated deeply with me. As the Caretaker, I've witnessed many narratives, but this was a raw testament to the human spirit's will to persevere even in the most harrowing of circumstances.

The corridor, with its countless tallies, ended at a solitary door, slightly ajar. I hesitated, but my curiosity won over. Pushing it open revealed a small, dimly lit room. In its center stood a skeletal figure, a chalk piece still clutched in its bony hand, the final mark etched onto the wall beside it. On the floor around it lay remnants of tattered clothes and an old, corroded water bottle.

A wave of sorrow washed over me. The individual had documented their journey till the very end, hoping, perhaps, that someone would find their story.

Retracing my steps, I pondered the weight of my role. Amidst this vast expanse of madness, was I merely a witness to the myriad tales of suffering? Or could I, in some way, bring solace, even if it was merely by acknowledging the stories of those long gone?

Shaking off the heaviness, I resumed my caretaking duties, the chalk marks serving as a somber reminder of the countless souls who had tried to conquer the Backrooms, only to be swallowed whole by its relentless labyrinth.

Entry 29: *I keep finding roses. Fresh and red. An anomaly in this decayed place.*

In the world of the Backrooms, where time seemed to lose meaning and the landscapes were an unending loop of desolation, anomalies stood out like an itch one couldn't scratch. Today's anomaly, though, was peculiarly poetic: roses.

I was navigating a serpentine hallway, its air thick with a musty scent and its floor peppered with worn-out tiles. I was engrossed in my cleaning, wiping away the grime from the yellowing walls, when my foot brushed against something soft. Looking down, my eyes met a striking contrast to the bleakness of my surroundings - a rose. Fresh, vibrant, its petals a brilliant shade of red, it lay on the ground as if someone had just dropped it. I stooped to pick it up, the velvety texture of its petals strikingly at odds with the cold, hard reality of the Backrooms.

A couple of corridors down, I found another. And then another. Like a trail of breadcrumbs in a twisted fairy tale, these roses seemed to beckon me, leading me onward. My mind wrestled with the bizarre reality of it. How could anything so fresh and alive exist in this place of decay and disrepair? The aroma was intoxicating, pulling me deeper into the labyrinth.

I began following the roses, picking up each one, forming a bouquet of rich crimson against the pallor of my surroundings. The ever-present hum of the fluorescent lights above seemed to diminish, replaced by the rhythmic beat of what sounded like a distant heart.

Eventually, I found myself standing before a vast ballroom, unlike any other space in the Backrooms. The opulent room, though still tinged with the characteristic yellow hue, had grand chandeliers hanging from its ceiling. Mirrors with ornate frames lined the walls, reflecting the eerie glow of the space. But the most striking feature was the center of the room: a large marble statue of a woman holding a bouquet of roses. Fresh, red roses.

As I approached the statue, a shiver ran down my spine. The statue's eyes, made of some gleaming gemstone, seemed almost lifelike. But it was the expression that haunted me — one of sorrow, longing, and a hint of malevolence. At the base of the statue, an inscription read, "To the Lost Loves of the Backrooms."

I carefully placed my bouquet with the rest, half expecting the statue to come alive. But nothing stirred, save for the silent, watchful eyes of the stone maiden. The roses, it seemed, were offerings to her — tokens of remembrance or perhaps appeasement.

Backing away slowly, I exited the ballroom, the vision etched into my memory. Was this statue an embodiment of the many souls trapped here? A representation of the heartache and despair? I couldn't say. But the stark juxtaposition of the decaying Backrooms with the fresh beauty of roses would remain one of the most unnerving experiences in my tenure as the Caretaker.

That night in my small room, as I tried to rest, the scent of roses invaded my senses, a sweet reminder of the strange enigma I had encountered. The Backrooms, it seemed, never ceased to surprise and confound me.

Entry 30: *Been hearing a song. A lullaby. Makes me drowsy. Need to resist.*

The vastness of the Backrooms often drowned its inhabitants in a cacophony of sounds, from the omnipresent buzzing of the fluorescent lights to the distant echoes of unidentifiable noises. Today, however, the soundscape was altered by the addition of a new element—a melody, soft and haunting.

As I made my way through a particularly lengthy corridor, I began to hear the faintest strains of a lullaby. It was delicate, almost ethereal in its composition, the kind of melody that, under normal circumstances, might have been comforting. But here, in the endless expanse of the Backrooms, it felt out of place, an unnerving juxtaposition to the otherwise harsh environment.

I tried to pinpoint the source of the song but it seemed to be coming from everywhere and nowhere at once. As I ventured deeper, the song grew louder, wrapping itself around me, seducing my senses. The gentle cadence, the soft hum, the lilting voice—all combined to create an aura of soporific tranquillity.

But the deeper the song penetrated my consciousness, the more drowsy I became. Every step felt like I was wading through treacle, my eyelids grew heavy, and an overwhelming desire to sleep tugged at the edges of my awareness. The very air seemed to be thick with a languorous haze, and the walls themselves pulsed gently to the rhythm of the lullaby.

I knew instinctively that succumbing to the song's allure would be a grave mistake. The Backrooms, with their shifting realities and lurking dangers, were no place to let one's guard down. Mustering all the strength I could, I tried to resist the song's pull, fighting the enveloping weariness with every ounce of willpower.

In an attempt to break the song's hold, I plugged my ears with bits of cloth torn from my shirt, but the lullaby persisted, echoing in my mind, a siren's call willing me into its embrace. Panic began to set in.

The notion of falling asleep and being vulnerable to whatever lurked in the Backrooms filled me with dread.

Desperation gave birth to an idea. Recalling a nearby room I had once cleaned, which had a rather loud, malfunctioning light fixture, I made my way there as quickly as my lethargic body would allow. The room's incessant electrical crackling was a harsh contrast to the gentle lullaby and, as hoped, began to drown out the song.

With the lullaby's grip weakening, my senses slowly started returning to normal. I stayed in that room, letting the sharp, erratic sounds of the faulty light fixture act as a barrier, shielding me from the lullaby's seductive trance, until I felt safe enough to venture out again.

As I continued my journey, the haunting notes of the lullaby grew fainter, eventually fading away entirely. But its memory lingered, a chilling reminder of the many traps and tests the Backrooms had in store for its inhabitants.

I often wondered after that day: Was the song a trap set by the Backrooms, or a remnant of a lost soul? Perhaps it was a combination of both, a siren's lullaby meant to ensnare the unwary. Whatever its origin, it was a grim testament to the fact that in the Backrooms, even beauty could be a weapon.

*Entry 31: **The white-dressed woman led me to a room. Full of keys. I took one. Feels important.***

For all the strange occurrences and shifting walls, today offered something entirely different—an encounter that might forever change my journey within the Backrooms. Wandering through yet another corridor, a distant figure caught my eye. A woman, dressed in a flowing white gown, her back turned to me. The fabric of her dress seemed to shimmer and flow, almost ethereal in nature, contrasting starkly against the dull, yellowed wallpaper that surrounded her.

I approached cautiously. In a place as unpredictable as this, it was never wise to trust appearances fully. But as I neared, she turned, her face obscured by a veil of white lace. Without uttering a word, she gestured for me to follow her. Intrigued, I did, feeling a strange pull towards her.

She led me through a maze of hallways, each more twisting and indistinct than the last. Just when I thought I'd lose myself to the labyrinth, she stopped in front of a peculiar door. Unlike the monotonous doors I'd grown accustomed to, this one was ornate, with intricate patterns and a worn-out golden handle.

Pushing it open, the sight that met me was unexpected. The room was vast and filled with rows upon rows of tables, and upon these tables lay thousands of keys. Each key was unique; some were rusty and ancient, others shiny and new, some looked like they belonged to diaries, while others seemed fit for grand gates.

The woman, her silent demeanor never wavering, glided towards the center of the room. With a delicate hand, she picked up a particular key and presented it to me. The key was a curious mix of old and new. Its blade was tarnished with age, while the bow was adorned with a fresh-looking blue gemstone that pulsed gently in the dim room.

As soon as I held it, a rush of emotions overwhelmed me—a mixture of hope, dread, and anticipation. It felt...significant. An object of purpose. Perhaps a key to a door I had yet to find, or maybe a puzzle piece to a riddle embedded within the Backrooms.

When I looked up to thank her or perhaps to question the key's importance, the woman had vanished, leaving me alone in the room with a sea of keys. I hastily exited, clutching the mysterious key tight in my grip, its cold metal warming slightly from the heat of my hand.

The encounter left me with more questions than answers. Who was this woman? Why lead me to this particular key? But above all, where does this key belong?

As I continued my journey, I made a mental note to be on the lookout for any door or lock that might fit this key. The Backrooms were full of mysteries, and this key was now a part of mine. The weight of potential in my pocket, I moved on, hoping to one day unravel the secrets it held.

Entry 32: *Watched a monster feed today. Horrifying. Yet, they seem to follow certain rules.*

My encounters with the monsters of the Backrooms have always been from a distance, a fleeting glimpse or a close call that I managed to escape from. But today, I witnessed something that was both chilling and oddly enlightening—something that will be etched in my memory for eternity.

The corridor seemed no different from countless others I'd traversed: the droning buzz of fluorescent lights, the yellowing wallpaper, and that ever-present sense of unease. As I rounded a corner, a guttural sound gave me pause. The noise was organic, fleshy, accompanied by muffled cries that sent shivers down my spine. Against my better judgment, I felt compelled to investigate, curiosity overpowering my innate sense of self-preservation.

Peering cautiously from behind an old wooden cabinet, I observed a grotesque scene. One of the monsters—its form shifting and indistinct, appearing as a mass of pulsating shadows—was crouched over a figure, a person, who was struggling weakly. The air was thick with the metallic scent of blood and the sharp tang of fear.

However, as I watched, paralyzed by a mixture of horror and fascination, I noticed something unexpected: a pattern, a ritual of sorts. The creature, instead of outright devouring its prey, seemed to engage in a dance. It would lean in, extending tendrils or appendages, making deliberate incisions, seemingly sampling different emotions or memories, before retreating. It was as if the creature was feeding not only on the physical being but on the very essence, the experiences, and emotions of its victim.

The process was slow, methodical, and strangely ceremonial. With each ebb and flow of this horrifying dance, the victim's struggles weakened, their cries softening to whimpers, and then silence. By the end, what remained was an empty husk—a body devoid of life and spirit.

Once the creature had its fill, it retreated into the shadows, disappearing as suddenly as it appeared, leaving behind the eerie quiet of the Backrooms and the remains of its feed.

I stumbled away, my stomach churning, my mind racing. These monsters, for all their apparent chaos and brutality, operated within certain boundaries, following rules or rituals known only to them. It begged the question: Were they simply mindless predators, or was there a deeper purpose, an intelligence or culture, governing their actions?

Gathering my wits, I continued on, now with a renewed sense of caution. The monsters of the Backrooms were not just random manifestations of fear; they had their own ways, their own mysteries. As the Caretaker, it was becoming increasingly clear that my role wasn't just to maintain order but to observe, learn, and perhaps one day, understand.

Entry 33: *The corridor stretched infinitely today. Had to turn back.*

Today, I faced an eeriness that managed to dwarf the countless oddities I've grown accustomed to during my tenure as the Caretaker.

I stepped into a corridor that I felt sure I'd traveled before. But as I began to walk, an overwhelming sense of disorientation gripped me. The path seemed to elongate with each step I took. The buzzing overhead lights seemed to blend into an infinite line, the monotonous yellow wallpaper stretching into eternity. Every few steps, the pattern of the wallpaper would repeat, as though it were a looping animation designed to unsettle and confuse.

At first, I attempted to rationalize the phenomenon, attributing it to fatigue or some trick of the light. But the longer I walked, the more I realized that my surroundings were genuinely warping. What should have been a short walk felt like miles, and the corridor never seemed to end.

I tried to mark my way using a piece of chalk from my bag, drawing a small 'X' on the wall. But as I continued my trek, that same 'X' would appear again and again at regular intervals. It was as if the corridor was folding into itself, resetting my progress with each step.

The air grew heavier, thick with a palpable sense of dread. Soft, distorted whispers seemed to emanate from the walls, a chorus of voices urging me to continue, to venture further into the never-ending void.

After what felt like hours, with no end in sight, panic began to take hold. I realized that if I didn't turn back, I might be trapped in this infinite loop forever. Ignoring the beckoning whispers, I retraced my steps, focusing on the sensation beneath my feet, the slight inconsistencies in the linoleum, anything to break the monotonous repetition of the corridor.

When I finally emerged, it felt as though a weight had been lifted off my shoulders. The endless corridor had been a test, a reminder that the Backrooms could warp not just space but perception itself. My role as the Caretaker had never seemed more crucial. For if I, with my knowledge and experience, could be ensnared by such a trap, what hope did the uninitiated have?

That night, as I settled into my makeshift resting spot, I made a note to avoid that corridor, marking it on one of my many maps. The Backrooms were a maze of anomalies, and while I had managed to escape this one, I knew that countless more awaited me in the shadows.

Entry 34: *Felt a breeze today. Fresh air? Followed it. Led to a brick wall. Mockery.*

The stifling, static-filled atmosphere of the Backrooms rarely gave way to anything resembling the comforts of the outside world. My senses, however dulled by the endless sameness, had become keenly attuned to even the slightest deviations. So when I felt that elusive sensation on my face—a gentle, cool breeze—it was as if a forgotten memory had come rushing back.

Eagerly, I followed the draft, a beacon in the lifeless void. Each step was filled with a mix of excitement and trepidation. My heart raced as the thought of fresh air, the world beyond the maze, filled my mind. Perhaps this was it, an exit or a window to the outside. Maybe, just maybe, the breeze was a signal that the Backrooms were finally allowing me respite.

As I journeyed through the labyrinthine corridors, I began to notice other anomalies—soft, rustling sounds like leaves in the wind, the distant chirping of birds, even the faintest trace of the scent of grass. Everything pointed to the tantalizing possibility of nature, something wild and untamed within these walls. The memories of open fields, cloudless blue skies, and the warmth of genuine sunlight fueled my determination.

But then, as the source of the breeze seemed to draw nearer, my surroundings took a more sinister turn. Wallpaper peeled away, revealing not the familiar yellow but a rough, bricked texture. Stains, old and fresh, smeared across the bricks, as if others had followed this path before and met a grim fate.

Finally, as I turned a corner, I found myself face to face with the source of the fresh air. It wasn't a window to the outside world, nor an exit from the eternal nightmare. Instead, a vast brick wall stood before me, a cruel mockery, a tangible testament to the Backrooms' ability to deceive and torment. Embedded in the wall was a small vent, barely the size of my fist, through which the tantalizing breeze flowed.

I collapsed to the ground, a mix of anger and despair flooding over me. My hopes, raised so high by the mere sensation of that breeze, were shattered in an instant. It was yet another trick, a game played by the Backrooms, reminding me of my captivity and my role as the Caretaker.

I sat there for what felt like hours, the gentle breeze a haunting reminder of what lay beyond my grasp. Eventually, I picked myself up, marking the location on my map to ensure I wouldn't fall for the same cruel trick again.

As I made my way back through the endless corridors, the realization hit me: The Backrooms were alive in their own way, feeding off hope, despair, and the souls trapped within. And as its Caretaker, I was both its keeper and its prisoner.

Entry 35: *The humming is getting louder. More oppressive.*

The seemingly infinite hallways of the Backrooms were never entirely silent. There was always the undercurrent of the electric buzz, the distant murmurs, and the subtle shiftings and groans of the place itself. However, as I navigated one such corridor, an unnatural stillness pervaded the air, sending shivers down my spine.

Rounding a corner, my body recoiled as I came face to face with a grotesque sight—an inert body, swaying slightly, suspended from the ceiling by a frayed rope. The dim, sickly-yellow glow of the overhead lights cast eerie shadows over the lifeless form, making the pale, decaying skin appear even more ghastly.

Despite the overwhelming urge to flee, something drew me closer, and I recognized the lifeless face—it was the other Caretaker I had encountered earlier. His once animated eyes now stared blankly ahead, devoid of life. His face, though twisted in a mask of despair, held a certain peace—a release from the relentless torment of the Backrooms.

Pinned to his dirtied shirt was a note, written with trembling hands on a stained piece of paper:

"I've clocked out. The endlessness, the games, the despair—it's too much. If you find this, know that this was my choice. My two-week notice to the Backrooms. Maybe freedom is possible after all."

The note's tragic finality weighed heavily on me. It was a sobering reminder that the mental toll of the Backrooms wasn't limited to the lost souls who stumbled upon this place. Even we, the supposed stewards, were vulnerable to its insidious influence.

Cautiously, I approached his cleaning cart, abandoned nearby. Among the familiar cleaning supplies were several objects of interest: a well-worn journal filled with hastily scribbled notes and maps detailing various areas of the Backrooms, some of which I had never encountered before.

Each entry provided a glimpse into the mind of a fellow Caretaker, charting his descent into despair. Some pages were filled with hope, detailing potential exits or safe zones. Others painted a grim picture, tales of close encounters with the monstrous denizens of the Backrooms, and the growing realization of the futility of his efforts. His maps, marked with annotations, symbols, and potential points of interest, held the potential to unlock new areas or provide insight into navigating the maze-like corridors.

With a heavy heart, I detached the note from his shirt and stowed away his journal and maps into my own bag. These resources could prove invaluable in navigating the treacherous paths of the Backrooms, perhaps even finding a way out. Or, at the very least, they could offer a glimmer of hope in an otherwise bleak existence.

I left the body as it was, a poignant reminder of the profound impact the Backrooms had on all its inhabitants, even its appointed guardians. As I continued on my path, a newfound determination surged within me—to honor the memory of the fallen Caretaker and to uncover the secrets that the Backrooms still held.

Entry 36: *Someone's been leaving breadcrumbs. Literal breadcrumbs. I decided to collect them.*

The pervasive dread that haunted the Backrooms had conditioned me to anticipate the unexpected, to find the eerie in the mundane. Yet nothing could have prepared me for the odd trail I stumbled upon today.

Trudging along a dim corridor, I noticed a minute irregularity against the monotony of the yellowed wallpaper and linoleum floors—small, crusty fragments scattered here and there. Bending down, I realized with a start that they were breadcrumbs.

An age-old tactic, I mused, recalling the tales of Hansel and Gretel. Had some lost soul used these crumbs as markers, attempting to trace their way back? The very thought of relying on something as ephemeral as breadcrumbs in this ever-changing labyrinth seemed both tragically hopeful and utterly foolish.

Yet as I followed the trail, my intrigue grew. The breadcrumbs appeared fresh, with no sign of decay or mold—a stark contrast to the timeless, rotting atmosphere of the Backrooms. Every so often, the breadcrumbs would form patterns: circles, arrows, and occasionally what looked like hastily drawn symbols. This wasn't just a path—it was a message, perhaps even a code.

With every breadcrumb I collected, a chilling sensation grew in the pit of my stomach. Whispers echoed faintly in the distance, becoming more pronounced as I progressed. It felt as though the very walls of the Backrooms were watching, gauging my reaction, toying with my senses.

After what felt like hours, the trail abruptly ended at a door unlike any I had encountered before. It was old, its wood warped and swollen from age, with faded paint peeling off in patches. Tied to its rusty handle was a small, tattered pouch, bulging with more breadcrumbs.

Cautiously, I approached, half-expecting some monstrous entity to burst forth. Instead, a note slipped out from the pouch, its handwriting desperate and hurried:

"They watch. They listen. The crumbs, my last hope. Collect them. They are more than they seem. Do not consume. Do not discard. Guard them."

The note's warning sent shivers down my spine. Without hesitation, I stowed the pouch safely in my bag, making a mental note to examine the breadcrumbs more closely when it was safer.

As I retraced my steps, I couldn't help but wonder about the person behind the breadcrumbs. Were they a friend or a foe? A victim of the Backrooms or another player in its twisted games? Regardless, one thing was certain: the breadcrumbs held a significance that went beyond simple navigation. They were a key, a puzzle piece in the vast enigma that was the Backrooms. And as the Caretaker, it was my duty to uncover their true purpose.

Entry 37: *Another shrine. Offered the breadcrumbs. Left feeling lighter.*

The vast expanse of the Backrooms has revealed many curiosities over time: twisted corridors, inexplicable rooms, and unending stretches of yellow wallpaper. But every now and then, I would stumble upon something even more enigmatic—shrines.

These shrines, often tucked away in obscure corners or hidden behind nondescript doors, were an amalgamation of lost relics, forgotten memories, and heartfelt offerings. Candles that never seemed to melt or go out, photographs faded with age, toys that had once brought joy to a child now lost, and an array of personal mementos, each telling a silent story of despair and hope.

Today, as I navigated a series of winding passages, the faint aroma of incense tickled my nostrils, guiding me towards another of these sanctuaries. Pushing open a creaking door, I found myself in a chamber bathed in a soft, ethereal glow. The walls were adorned with intricate tapestries depicting sorrowful figures and eerie landscapes. In the center stood an ornate altar, draped in red and gold cloth, with a myriad of offerings laid out: coins, trinkets, and handwritten notes.

Remembering the breadcrumbs I had collected, and the weight of their unexplained importance, I approached the shrine with reverence. As I placed the pouch gently on the altar, a strange sensation washed over me. It was as if the very essence of the Backrooms acknowledged the breadcrumbs, embracing them as part of its enigma.

Moments later, a profound stillness settled in the room. The constant buzzing of the fluorescent lights, which had become the soundtrack of my existence, faded into nothingness. The oppressive weight of the Backrooms, its ever-present gloom and melancholy, momentarily lifted. It was a fleeting respite, a brief moment of serenity that felt alien yet deeply comforting.

As I exited the chamber, the sense of lightness persisted. It was as though the breadcrumbs, in their offering, had absorbed a portion of the Backrooms' malevolence, granting me a temporary shield against its torment.

But with this newfound clarity came unsettling questions. Who had crafted these shrines? Were they merely a coping mechanism for lost souls, or did they serve a more profound purpose? Did they hold the power to influence the very fabric of the Backrooms? Only time, and my continued exploration, would tell.

Entry 38: *The keys! They're a puzzle. Found a door with multiple locks today. Will come back.*

Navigating the labyrinthine world of the Backrooms can be monotonous—a seemingly never-ending cycle of flickering lights, musty corridors, and that persistent hum that never quite fades into the background. But every once in a while, something would break the tedium, throwing me into a swirl of intrigue and apprehension. Today, that something was a door.

It wasn't like the other nondescript doors that adorned the Backrooms. This one was ancient, grand, and seemingly out of place—a massive wooden door, its timeworn surface etched with intricate patterns and symbols. Faded runes and glyphs, some eerily familiar and others completely alien, danced around the perimeter. But what caught my attention the most was the multitude of locks that secured it. There were at least a dozen, each unique in design, ranging from rusty iron padlocks to more sophisticated contraptions that seemed out of time and place.

Recalling the key I had previously acquired from the room the white-dressed woman led me to, I felt an urge to approach, an almost magnetic pull. The key was old, with peculiar notches and patterns. Tentatively, I tried it in one of the locks. To my astonishment, there was a soft click, and the lock came undone.

A rush of excitement surged through me, but then reality set in. One lock was now open, but there were many more to conquer. The implication was clear: this door, with its myriad of locks, was a puzzle waiting to be solved. It seemed that scattered throughout the Backrooms were keys, each holding the potential to unlock another piece of this grand enigma.

I spent hours at the door, studying each lock, hoping for clues. But as the ever-present weight of the Backrooms pressed on me, I decided to retreat, vowing to come back. I needed more keys, and possibly more knowledge. There were symbols on the door that seemed important—maybe they were hints or perhaps warnings.

As I made my way back to my makeshift base, my mind raced with possibilities. What lay beyond the door? Salvation? Another layer of the Backrooms? Or perhaps something darker, something that had been intentionally locked away? The allure of the unknown tugged at me, but so did the fear of what might be unleashed.

It became clear that my journey in the Backrooms had evolved. No longer was I merely a caretaker or a lost soul wandering aimlessly. I had a mission now, a purpose. The door and its secrets beckoned, and I was determined to unravel its mysteries—one key at a time.

Entry 39: *I think the monsters know about the door. They're guarding it.*

For all its unnerving peculiarities, the Backrooms had a rhythm to it—a twisted form of equilibrium that oscillated between eerie calm and palpable tension. Today, however, that rhythm was disrupted. The atmosphere felt charged, almost electric. The usual hum that underscored the corridors was heightened, infused with an insidious resonance that set my nerves on edge.

Upon approaching the corridor leading to the enigmatic door, it was immediately evident something had changed. Shadows danced in the periphery, their forms ethereal and fleeting. The already dim lights seemed dimmer, casting a malevolent amber glow. But it was the presence of the monsters that was the most jarring.

They lined the corridor, their forms more pronounced than I had ever seen them before. It wasn't just the usual grotesque figures either—there were others, creatures I hadn't encountered in my time here. Some were tall and spindly, with elongated limbs ending in razor-sharp claws, while others were stout and hulking, their forms shrouded in tattered cloaks that failed to hide the malevolence beneath.

While I had managed to strike a delicate balance with some of these creatures in the past, this felt different. Their usual aimless wandering was replaced by deliberate positioning. It was clear they were guarding the door, as if alerted to my prior discovery.

Venturing closer, their reactions varied. Some turned their hollow eyes towards me, emanating a chilling aura, while others growled, the sound echoing in the confined space of the corridor. A few whispered among themselves, their voices melding into a cacophony of hisses and murmurs, like a sinister symphony playing just for me.

I contemplated confronting them, but quickly realized that without all the keys, any such encounter would be futile. I needed more information, more resources, and perhaps even allies.

Retreating was the wise choice, but it didn't come without its challenges. A few of the monsters, perhaps more curious than others, decided to give chase. Darting through corridors, I found myself drawing upon knowledge gained from the maps and journals I had acquired, using them to weave a path of escape, leading the creatures into looping rooms and endless hallways.

Once certain I had lost them, I sought refuge in one of the less-traveled areas of the Backrooms. Panting and drenched in cold sweat, I contemplated my next move. The door's significance was now undeniable—not just to me, but to the denizens of this maze as well.

If the monsters felt threatened by the potential of what lay behind the door, then perhaps it held the key to altering the very fabric of the Backrooms. Whatever its secret, the path to unlocking it was now fraught with even more danger.

As I settled down, attempting to gain some rest in the unnerving silence, a singular thought dominated my mind: the game had changed. And if I wasn't careful, the next move could very well be my last.

Entry 40: *Deeper and deeper I go. There's a pull, a gravity to this place.*

The Backrooms seemed to be built on layers of contradiction. While the endless, identical hallways screamed stagnation, there was a dynamic undercurrent, an unspoken pull that subtly directed one's journey. And now, that pull was no longer subtle.

It was the kind of gravitational tug you'd feel when standing at the edge of a precipice, tempted by the void below. Every step I took was deliberate, yet it felt like I was being guided, or rather, compelled, deeper into the labyrinth. The familiar scent of stale air and old wallpaper grew increasingly potent, replaced intermittently by something more primal, an earthy aroma reminiscent of wet soil and moss.

The once omnipresent, monotonous yellow walls began to change. They started displaying patches of deep green, then slowly, whole corridors were draped in moss and creeping vines. The linoleum floors, worn and stained from decades of existence, gave way to soft, damp earth that squelched underfoot.

The light fixtures overhead became fewer, their incessant buzzing growing distant, replaced by an ambient luminescence emitted from bioluminescent fungi that clung to the walls and ceiling. Their gentle glow painted the surroundings in shades of blue and green, casting eerie shadows that danced with every flicker.

And with this descent into a more organic realm, the ambient sounds changed too. The oppressive silence was occasionally broken by the distant sound of dripping water, the soft rustling of leaves, and the faint, echoing calls of creatures unknown.

The monsters I had become accustomed to seemed scarcer in these parts. In their place, I encountered other entities—shapes that lurked just beyond the reach of the bioluminescent glow, observing from the shadows. Some resembled animals, but twisted, with too many eyes or limbs that moved unnaturally. Others were more humanoid but remained elusive, vanishing before I could get a good look.

As I ventured deeper, I stumbled upon clearings, spaces where the ceilings stretched high and openings allowed for cascades of underground waterfalls. Around these water sources, strange plants thrived—some with pulsing veins and others that seemed to hum a tune, almost beckoning me closer.

But the pull, that irresistible force, didn't want me to linger. It guided me towards a specific direction—a heart of this organic realm. I felt it in my bones, a resonance, a call that was hard to resist.

Amidst this subterranean jungle, I found a colossal tree. Its trunk was gnarled and twisted, its roots intertwining with the very fabric of the Backrooms. From its sprawling branches hung various objects: old lanterns, shoes, pieces of clothing, and more disturbingly, bones. As if everything and everyone eventually got drawn to this ancient sentinel.

The pull was strongest here. Leaning against the tree trunk, I could hear its whispers, ancient and profound. It spoke of times before the Backrooms, of lost souls and gateways. Was this tree the epicenter of this place? A guardian or perhaps a prisoner?

Though tempted to stay and decipher its mysteries, the inherent dangers of this newfound depth were not lost on me. For now, I marked the location in the journal, vowing to return, to uncover the secrets that this ancient behemoth held.

But one thing was clear: The Backrooms, as vast and infinite as they seemed, had depths yet to be discovered, each layer more mysterious and intriguing than the last. And I, the Caretaker, was inexorably linked to its ever-unfolding enigma.

Entry 41: *Lights went out completely today. The darkness is alive.*

In the ever-twisting maze of the Backrooms, there were constants I had come to depend on. The incessant hum of the lights, the all-encompassing golden glow, the undercurrent of stale, unmoving air. But today, that changed.

Without warning, the world plunged into an abyss of absolute darkness. It was so sudden that my eyes didn't have time to adjust, nor could they. This wasn't the gentle, forgiving darkness of a night without moonlight; this was the cold, unyielding blackness of a sealed coffin.

A wave of panic surged over me. My first instinct was to scramble for my flashlight, but even its beam seemed swallowed, absorbed by the thick obsidian void around me. The very concept of direction became meaningless. I took tentative steps, feeling out my surroundings. The familiar linoleum beneath my feet felt different, almost squishy, like damp moss.

But it wasn't just the tactile world that had shifted. The silence of the Backrooms was shattered. In this palpable blackness, a symphony of whispers came to life, rising and falling in an indecipherable cacophony. There was a weight to the air, a pressure against my eardrums, as if the very darkness had substance and intent.

But the most unsettling realization was that this darkness wasn't just an absence of light. It moved. Shapes, more like shifting voids within voids, passed by me—some at a distance and others uncomfortably close. A chilling brush against my arm or the sensation of something moving just past my face became regular occurrences.

I felt watched, not by eyes, but by an awareness. The very fabric of this shadowy realm seemed conscious, observing and reacting to my presence. At one point, I was sure I felt a hand, cold and insubstantial, briefly grasp mine, only to vanish a moment later.

To keep my sanity, I began to hum—a feeble attempt to combat the oppressive weight of the whispers and to reassure myself of my own existence. My voice sounded muffled, as if the darkness was trying to swallow it, just as it had swallowed the light.

Hours or perhaps mere minutes passed—it was impossible to tell. The concept of time became irrelevant. The only thing that mattered was the growing urge to find a way out, to escape the suffocating embrace of this sentient void.

As hope dwindled, a distant, dim light began to emerge. A glimmer, a pinprick in the vast canvas of black. Drawn to it like a moth to a flame, I hastened my pace. The light grew brighter and more defined. It wasn't the familiar fluorescent glow of the Backrooms, but a soft, silvery luminescence.

Emerging from the inky blackness, I found myself in a vast chamber bathed in moonlight filtering down from some unseen source above. The chamber's floor was covered in silver sand, and in the center stood a tall, ornate mirror with a frame carved in intricate patterns.

Cautiously approaching the mirror, I saw my own reflection. But behind me, in the darkness I had just exited, countless eyes stared back—each one glinting with a malevolent intelligence. The realization hit me: the darkness was never just a lack of light. It was a living, breathing entity, a hive of countless beings observing, studying, and perhaps waiting for the right moment.

I hurried away from the chamber, a renewed sense of urgency pushing me forward. The Backrooms had shown me yet another facet of its enigmatic nature, a reminder that even the seemingly familiar could turn treacherous. The rules were constantly changing, and I, the Caretaker, was merely a player in its grand, inscrutable design.

Entry 42: *I found the boy from the shoe. He's one of them now.*

Throughout my tenure as the Caretaker, my encounters with remnants of lost souls had been rather impersonal. An article of clothing, a scribbled note, the distant wail or laughter echoing through the labyrinth. But today was different. Today, I found the boy.

A few entries ago, I had mentioned stumbling upon a child's shoe, bloodied and forlorn. A shiver had coursed through me then, thinking of the child it once belonged to, hoping against hope that he had somehow found an exit. My wishes were naive, I realize now.

As I wandered the interminable corridors, I heard soft, melodic humming. Drawn to it, I turned a corner into a dimly lit section, the bulbs overhead flickering sporadically, casting the corridor in a dance of light and shadow. There, in the midst of this dance, stood a young boy, no older than ten. The humming emanated from him, but it was the gleam in his eyes that arrested my attention: they shone an unnatural shade of electric blue, pulsating with an eerie light.

I approached cautiously, noticing that he wore a mismatched shoe, the mate to the bloodied one I had found. He didn't acknowledge my approach, continuing to hum, but as I got closer, the tune became clearer—it was a children's lullaby, distorted and off-key, sending icy tendrils of dread down my spine.

"Hey, kid," I ventured, voice shaking. "Are you alright?"

He stopped humming and turned to face me fully. His skin, once probably a healthy shade of youthful tan, was now a ghostly pale, nearly translucent. Dark veins webbed across his face, branching out like tendrils of decay. His clothes were tattered, smeared with streaks of dried blood and other unidentifiable substances.

But it was his eyes that held me captive. They glowed even brighter now, and within them swirled a maelstrom of emotions—pain, confusion, rage. "I lost my shoe," he said, voice devoid of any emotion, pointing to his mismatched feet.

"I... I found it," I stammered, trying to keep my composure. "But what happened to you?"

A slow smile spread across his face, but it was devoid of warmth or happiness. Instead, it was a grotesque parody, revealing teeth that had grown too sharp for a child's mouth. "They found me," he whispered. "Now, I'm one of them."

With a swiftness that belied his appearance, he lunged at me, fingers elongated into claws. I barely managed to dodge and, not waiting to see if he would pursue, ran as fast as my legs would carry me.

When I dared to look back, he was gone, but his haunting lullaby continued to echo through the corridors. The grim realization weighed heavily on my heart: the Backrooms had claimed another victim, twisting innocence into something nightmarish. This place was not just a maze; it was a transformer of souls. And if a child could be turned, who was to say I wasn't next?

Entry 45: *The woman in white warned me. "Not all exits lead out."*

The whispers had quieted, the relentless hum of the lights was my only companion in this stretch of the Backrooms. It was during this brief moment of solitude, as I dutifully wiped an old wooden table clean of some unidentifiable substance, that I saw her.

The woman in white.

She stood a few feet away from me, framed by an old-fashioned doorway, her long white dress flowing around her like tendrils of mist. She seemed almost ethereal, with the pallor of her skin contrasting sharply against the darkness of the room behind her. Her face, as always, was partially obscured, with her flowing hair cascading like a waterfall in front of her eyes.

I hesitated for a moment, but her presence had never brought harm. Still, every encounter was an enigma, and this was no exception. Before I could make a move, she spoke, her voice a haunting whisper that seemed to come from all directions, "Not all exits lead out."

The weight of her words settled in the pit of my stomach. In a place filled with misleading doorways and trap-laden passages, her warning was dire. The urge to flee, to find an escape, was always present. But her cautionary words hinted at darker consequences for picking the wrong path.

"Why?" I finally managed to ask, my voice echoing in the vastness of the Backrooms. "Why tell me this? Why are you so interested in me?"

She took a step closer, the shadows dancing around her, her face still shrouded in mystery. "You are not like the others. You tend to this place. You see beyond the surface. You hold the balance between the lost souls and the creatures that lurk. That makes you valuable... and vulnerable."

The thought had never occurred to me. In the complexity of my role, the idea that I was somehow special or unique had never crossed my mind. Yet her words resonated with an undeniable truth.

"But what do you want from me?" I pressed, trying to decipher her intentions.

Her silhouette shifted as if she was tilting her head, considering her response. "I once was like you, bound to this place, nurturing its vastness. But time erodes even the strongest of wills. I am here to guide, to caution, and perhaps... to atone."

Her words, laced with melancholy, hung in the air for a brief moment before she began to fade, her form dissipating into a fine mist. But before she vanished entirely, I heard her say, "Remember, not all exits lead out. Choose wisely."

The room returned to its usual dimmed state. The woman in white was gone, leaving me with more questions than answers. My role as the Caretaker became more intricate with each passing day, but her guidance, however cryptic, provided a beacon of hope in the twisted maze that was the Backrooms. But one thing was clear: to navigate this place, I would need more than just intuition. I needed knowledge.

Entry 48: *Today was calm. Too calm. Preparing for....something big.*

The eerie silence of the Backrooms today was palpable, a stark contrast to the usual haunting symphony of murmurs, echoes, and the ever-present hum of fluorescent lights. Long stretches of the honeycombed, yellow wallpapered corridors lay before me, uninterrupted by the usual anomalies.

I moved cautiously, my cleaning cart squeaking in protest with each turn of its wheel. My encounters with the entities that inhabit these endless halls had always been fraught with danger, but today, there was no sign of them. No skittering shadows or fleeting glimpses of grotesque figures. The silence was omnipresent, only broken by my own tentative footsteps.

It was then, amidst this hush, that I saw a figure at the end of one of the hallways. Humanoid in shape, but the details were obscure, obscured by a sort of wavering mirage effect. I approached carefully, and as I drew nearer, the figure became clearer, revealing an individual I had only heard rumors of – a Backrooms designer.

He was tall and gaunt, dressed in a timeless, tattered ensemble, complete with a vest and bowtie. Around his waist was a toolbelt filled with an assortment of odd instruments, some of which emitted a gentle glow. But it was his eyes that captivated me the most, ancient and knowledgeable, holding centuries of secrets.

"You're wondering about the silence, aren't you?" he began, his voice a soft whisper, yet carrying an authority that made me stand at attention.

I nodded, unable to find my voice.

"The Backrooms are changing, evolving. What you've seen, what you've experienced, is just the tip of the iceberg," he continued, gesturing to the surroundings.

I cleared my throat. "Are you... Are you responsible for this?"

He chuckled, a low and mirthless sound. "We, the designers, merely shape the parameters. The Backrooms have a consciousness of their own."

The corridor suddenly began to shift, the walls elongating, and the ceiling stretching upwards. He seemed unfazed. "You've been chosen, Caretaker. Chosen to bear witness to the next phase."

He reached into his vest and produced a key, ornate and shimmering, and handed it to me. "When the time comes, you'll know what to do."

As suddenly as he had appeared, the designer began to fade, his form blurring and merging with the ever-shifting walls of the Backrooms.

I was left alone, the weight of his words pressing down on me. I looked down at the key in my hand, its surface etched with intricate patterns. What door would it open? What horrors, or perhaps salvation, lay beyond?